Everything and Nothing

***

Ola Ademola-Adesanoye

Accomplish Press

www.accomplishpress.com

First published in 2022 in the United Kingdom by

Accomplish Press Ltd, Kemp House, 152 City Road, London EC1V 2NX

www.accomplishpress.com

Paperback Edition published in 2022

All characters appearing in this work are fictitious.

Any resemblance to real persons, living or dead is purely coincidental.

Cover Design: Pixelstudio

CONTENTS

CHAPTER 1

Bibi felt the coolness of the gentle breeze through her Bottega Veneta ribbed polo top as she strolled down the high street. Her light pink cardigan made from pure wool was tied around her slender waist. She briefly contemplated putting it on but decided against it. She wanted to enjoy the brisk weather just a little longer. An absolute euphoric feeling raked through her body as she floated on cloud nine.

Bibi adored the spectrum of bright leaf colours, from green to vivid red, crimson, scarlet, or even orange. Autumn was definitely her favourite time of the year.

After a few minutes of walking, she arrived at her favourite café and chose a high stool by the large, floor to ceiling window. The view was perfect for what she liked to do best; people watch. She particularly enjoyed trying to tell the stories of people as they walked by, but today, everyone seemed to be in a rush or on their phones as they hurried past.

A hard read today. She gave up.

Bibi hummed softly and smiled to herself as she pulled her light pink cardigan tighter around her. Then she sipped her coffee and waited patiently for her friend, Naomi, to arrive.

Naomi was hardly ever on time for anything, within their circle of friends, she was often referred to as the perpetual latecomer.

"Hey, you!" Naomi squealed in her loud, bubbly voice as she came up behind Bibi. Bibi almost jumped out of her chair. Regaining her composure, she rose to hug her friend. Bibi was glad she didn't spill coffee on her expensive polo top. She kept that thought to herself, for fear of coming across too vain.

"You kept me waiting, again," Bibi said, trying to pull a mean face.

"I am so sorry. Believe it or not, I did set out early but got caught up in the rush hour traffic. I will make it up to you, I promise," Naomi answered with an amiable smile. Naomi had a big personality with a contagious smile and always seemed happy. This made her hard to resist. Bibi could hardly stay mad at Naomi because she could not resist Naomi's positivity.

"Apology accepted," Bibi said, "Would you like a drink?"

"Thank you, I am alright for now. We can grab a bite later if you are okay for time?"

Naomi took off her jumper, neck scarf, and set about making herself comfortable, even as she continued to study Bibi carefully. She couldn't place her finger on it, but Bibi seemed different. Pulling out a stool and just as she was about to sit on it, it struck her! Bibi was glowing with excitement.

"Spill it, girl, I can feel the excitement radiating off you, why do you look so happy?" Naomi asked.

"Make yourself comfortable girlfriend, you will be needing a drink for this part," Bibi replied in a sing-song voice, intentionally looking away while still grinning from ear to ear like a Cheshire cat.

She needed to milk every part of this!

"So, how's your mom doing?" Bibi asked Naomi.

"Don't you even think of distracting me," Naomi said to her sternly.

Bibi pretended to sulk. Naomi, never one to acquiesce easily, paused for a second then changed tactics.

Smiling sweetly, she said softly "Okay, please tell me why you sounded so excited on the phone. I will beg you if I must but don't make me though".

Bibi rolled her eyes before laying her left hand purposefully on the dark brown oak table. Naomi sighed and rolled her eyes too. Perhaps Bibi would tell her what was going on with her when she was ready. Glancing around briefly, Naomi thought she saw a glint of something sparkly out of the corner of her right eye. She looked away but instantly looked back.

Naomi yelped, leapt out of her seat, and did a little spinning dance. Then, suddenly aware of her surroundings, she calmed down and sat back down. "My friend just got engaged!" she said, beaming broadly at a passing waitress.

"Well, congratulations," the waitress said to Bibi.

"Thank you," Bibi replied, blushing with embarrassment. She wanted to crawl under the table and hide.

"Goodness gracious, he did it! That man finally did it!" Naomi said under her breath. She walked around the table and hugged Bibi.

"Well, let me see how good he did," Naomi said, reaching for Bibi's left hand to admire the stunning emerald cut halo engagement ring.

Simply exquisite.

It sat perfectly on Bibi's slender ring finger!

Bibi smiled. She still remembered the day Naomi had introduced her to Ken. It was at a house party Naomi was throwing to welcome Ken home from his time overseas working with a Christian missionary network. His homecoming just also happened to coincide with his 30th birthday, and Naomi had managed to rope Bibi in.

She was standing by the buffet table when her eyes met his mesmerising gaze from across the room for the very first time. He revealed a sparkling set of white teeth when he smiled at her, and his eyes drank in hers as their eyes locked. *Man, this guy is fly,* she thought to herself. She had already seen pictures of him that Naomi had shown her but seeing him in person was so much better. She thought his pictures did not even do him justice.

His long-sleeved white linen top and indigo blue jeans suited him to a tee. His toned arms were just the right size, not those oversized bulging biceps that every guy seemed to have these days. It just wasn't her taste.

The attraction she felt was intense. It had a magnetic pull, and Bibi's heart was racing rapidly as she felt a jittery sensation in the pit of her stomach. Across the room, Ken's palms were clammy, and he couldn't focus on anything else. Aware of what was happening, he quickly looked away, though he couldn't stop smiling. Bibi looked down and brushed the invisible crumbs from her dress. When she looked up, Ken was gone.

"I see you've met Ken," Naomi said, coming to stand beside Bibi.

"Um, not really, no."

"Girl, I was watching you drooling over him just minutes ago," Naomi teased.

"I was not drooling," Bibi whispered harshly.

"Yes, you were," Naomi replied, chuckling.

"So, should I introduce you to him?" Naomi asked Bibi, looking serious now.

"Yes, I would like that," Bibi said without hesitation.

But before Naomi could do her little victory dance, Bibi grabbed her by the elbow and led her out to the patio.

They stood side by side in silence for a little while. Bibi loved the feel of the gentle breeze against her face. "Tell me again, Naomi, who is this guy and how do you know him?"

"We practically grew up together, Bibi. Our moms have been best friends since I was eight years old. I would never introduce you to him if he were not a good guy. Trust me, he is all that and more."

Bibi was going to ask Naomi why she had not snagged him herself if he was that great of a guy, but then she remembered that he was not Naomi's cup of tea.

Bibi listened as Naomi went on to reiterate how her mother Shona and Ken's mother, Mabel, had met.

Mabel had knocked on Shona's door with a welcome hamper years ago, when Naomi and her family first moved into the neighbourhood, and the two women had hit it off at once. Naomi's family had moved next door to Ken and his family when they first arrived in the United Kingdom from Haiti. Ken and Naomi became close because of their mothers' friendship.

"I spoke little English at the time, so it was the perfect opportunity for us to hang out together, me and Ken. It was a match made in heaven. I needed to improve my English and Ken's grade in French was slipping."

Bibi nodded and nudged Naomi to continue. She had heard bits and pieces of the story of Ken and Naomi over the last year, but for some reason, seeing him in the flesh had triggered a need for her to get a refresher.

"I was enrolled at the same primary school that Ken attended. After we finished primary school, we ended up going to different high schools, but we stayed in touch and kept our relationship intact. Even after my mom and I moved twenty minutes away after she and my dad divorced, we stayed close to Ken and his family."

"What happened to your dad? I don't think I've ever heard this part of the story," Bibi said. Bibi turned to face Naomi this time and noticed Naomi's face wore a sombre expression.

Naomi sighed before she continued. "My dad moved back to Haiti. Over the years, Ken and I became close, he's like a brother to me. He was the first person I told at sixteen that I am a lesbian. He gently coaxed me to tell my parents and friends and supported me through that challenging time as I faced adversity and discrimination."

Bibi nodded as she took her hand in hers and gently squeezed it, to reassure her. Naomi smiled at Bibi before making her way back in.

Bibi leaned gently against the patio doors, lost in her thoughts. She herself had sometimes wondered if she would have been friends with Naomi had she known about her sexual orientation before they became friends. Honestly, it may have clouded her judgement, but she would never know now. Homosexuality is simply not an acceptable way of life in Nigeria. In Nigeria, it is an offence punishable with jail time. So, she had struggled with her thoughts when she first realised that Naomi was gay. And even now, she sometimes finds herself mulling over it.

It helps that Naomi is a loyal and very selfless person. It made her easy to love, and Bibi had come to accept that this was just who her best friend was. Others didn't quite see things the same way. Even so, a few of Bibi's Nigerian friends on campus had been indifferent, some quite opposed to her friendship with Naomi, and were quite hostile about it. Bibi could not understand how they could claim to be Christians and be that judgemental. Particularly, when a young, married father, who was also a highly respected member of their church in Nigeria, now living with his girlfriend off-campus. Not only that, but he had also moved in with her only two months after arriving in the UK on a missionary scholarship. The last time he ran into her and Naomi at the library, he had glared at them so hard that she felt like his eyes were going to dig a hole right through her. Then he had hurled offensive words at them. Just thinking back on that incident made her shudder.

Hypocrisy in her books!

But it still did not stop her from questioning if she should be friends with Naomi.

She and Naomi had first met months ago, on their first day of class. Bibi had just arrived in England two weeks prior, for her post-graduate degree at the Queen Mary University of London, which is one of England's prestigious universities. It was also where her mom and dad had studied many decades ago. On that first day of class, Naomi had scurried into class, running late, and hurried to occupy the vacant seat beside Bibi. Naomi had smiled nervously before settling down.

Bibi was astounded by Naomi's beauty. A black girl with blue eyes? She was instantly drawn to her. They had quickly become inseparable. As their friendship blossomed, Bibi would come to find out that Naomi was not wearing contact lenses on the day they had met.

The first time Naomi had mentioned Ken was when Bibi accompanied her to the post office, to send him his favourite goodies while he was abroad working with 'New Smiles,' a global Christian missionary network that provides free reconstructive surgery and dental care to children with cleft lips and cleft palate. He had been away for a while working across six countries.

The party was lively and fun. The food spread included Bibi's Nigerian jollof rice and coleslaw that everyone seemed to enjoy; Naomi's pork griot and her mom's homemade pikliz as perfect sides. K.J, another friend, manned the barbeque stand with an array of various delicacies; corn on the cob, burgers, sausages, and fish. The aroma that wafted from the sizzling spread was mouth-watering and tantalising. There was an endless flow of drinks as well, as were several delicious desserts to choose from. Ken's mom made the cake, her signature flavour, red velvet, and it tasted divine. Bibi especially had a weakness for cakes and that day, she had more slices than she should have had, she could not resist.

After her conversation with Naomi on the patio, Bibi was now even more intrigued by Ken. His was the first face she sought when she walked back into the party. She spotted him in the corner, chatting with a male and female friend. Their eyes met again, this time only briefly, as if he was acknowledging her presence before continuing his conversation.

Throughout the rest of the evening, she could sense Ken's glances now and then. Even when ladies were busy flirting with him, he paid them compliments smiling, yet respectfully maintained his distance.

Playing the hostess alongside Naomi, Bibi watched him through the corner of her eyes. They both smiled each time their eyes met, and she loved the feeling of butterflies in her stomach that came with each stolen glance. She felt giddy and smiled throughout the night. Bibi was glad she had paid extra attention to her outfit and makeup. She had worn one of her form-fitting floral maxi dresses that hugged her in the right places in a graceful and sexy way.

Eventually, when the party was winding down, Ken made his way across the room to the patio, where Bibi had finally retreated to rest her aching feet. She watched as he was stopped a few times by friends and cousins asking him about his trip and future. The last person to interrupt his journey towards her was Naomi, who was animatedly pointing in Bibi's direction. Bibi looked away, not wanting to seem eager. She knew Naomi was telling him to approach her, which he eventually did.

"Mimi has told me so much about you," he said when he finally got to her. His rich, baritone voice sounded so melodious that Bibi could hardly breathe. "I feel like I know you already. May I sit?" He asked, gesturing at the chair across the small patio table from her.

Bibi nodded. Normally, she would have berated herself for not saying something, but something told her that with Ken, she could be herself. It did not matter, and for some reason, she didn't feel silly, just a sense of thrill.

"I've been waiting to be alone with you all evening," he said, gazing into her eyes.

"Same here," she whispered, her eyes meeting his. His eyes were a hue of azure with a hint of grey, and she had never seen freckles suit anyone as much as they did Ken. It was the first time she was seeing his face clearly all evening, and she liked what she saw. Before her, sat a tall, good-looking man with a posture that screamed confidence.

Later that evening, Ken asked Bibi to dance with him. She stood up and felt a little rush go to her head. She shook off the lightheaded feeling because she was excited to finally be close to Ken. Close enough to him that she could smell his scent, it had a slight hint of musk and cedarwood. The scent was exhilarating and rousing! She could even feel the hairs on the back of her neck standing.

After everyone left, she and Naomi had to finish cleaning up. Ken stayed back to help. When they were done, Naomi retired to bed, leaving the two of them on her sofa, where they talked into the wee hours of the morning. Ken was easy to talk to and open-minded. They had quite a bit in common and she enjoyed listening to his stories from his work abroad. She loved that he listened to her stories and was interested in them too. Ken also loved music. They both had an affinity to jazz and contemporary gospel music. At one point during the night, he fetched a throw for her when she felt a little cold. He even went the extra mile and made her a cup of hot cocoa with marshmallows. Little, thoughtful things. Bibi felt right at home with him.

CHAPTER 2

"**M**om, she said yes! Did you hear me? I am getting married to the most gorgeous girl on earth." Ken was grinning so hard that his mother could not help but smile too. It warmed her heart to see him so happy.

"I still feel like I am dreaming and, sometimes, I feel like I am punching above my weight."

"I heard you, son, and I am so happy for you. Congratulations! For the record, any lady will be lucky to have you. She comes across as down to earth regardless of the affluence and old money she was born into."

"Mom, she is. Bibi really is!"

Ken's mother, Mabel, walked around the kitchen island to hug her son. She held him so tightly that he felt he might choke.

Pulling away, he heard his mother's sniffles.

"Don't cry, mom, this is great news!"

"It is. These are happy tears," she said, touching the side of his face.

Ken smiled and hugged his mother back. He sometimes marvelled at how women could cry over anything, even happy news. Even Bibi had cried when he proposed to her. The truth be told, he held back a tear or two that memorable day too. How could he not? It had meant the world to him that he asked her to marry him and that she said yes. He had planned every single detail. Everything had gone just the way he had imagined it would, how could he not get emotional over something like that?

He looked at his mother wiping the tears from her cheek and smiled.

She caught him watching her and chuckled.

"So, tell me all about it, Ken," Mabel said, taking a seat on the kitchen stool.

Ken leaned his upper body on the island, his heart skipping a beat, as he thought back to the day he had proposed.

He had let himself into Bibi's apartment that Friday evening, knowing she was at the school library, swotting for an upcoming exam paper. Thankfully, for the short window of time he had, he only had to put up the décor, order her favourite Thai meal and iced tea for delivery. They had shared their first kiss at her favourite Thai restaurant, so he knew this setting would be memorable.

Bibi had spoken endlessly about her dream of visiting all the ancient temples in Chiang Mai one day. Maybe, their honeymoon destination.

Before showing up at her apartment, Ken had spent hours practising his speech in front of a mirror at home. Even so, he was so nervous that his words tumbled out when the time came to spill them out to Bibi.

None of that mattered in the end because Bibi was hysterical with tears and laughter by the time he was done. He was sure she had not heard a word, and neither did she seem to care. It was the gesture that counted the most. Him, on his knee; ring in his hand, eyes locked, words coming out of his mouth. She said yes, over, and over. It was all so surreal, and intimate.

"So, how did you pick out the perfect ring?" Mabel asked.

Chuckling as he remembered how mortified he had been when the shop assistant asked for her ring size, he looked at his mother and admitted he did not know what he was doing at the time.

"I went looking at rings but completely forgot that I would need her ring size," Ken said.

Mabel smiled and shook her head.

"I had to get Mimi to help me."

"I'm surprised she was able to keep it a secret," Mabel said, laughing lightly.

"Well, me too," Ken admitted, "I was so nervous the entire time thinking, Mimi wouldn't be able to hold it and might spoil the surprise, but she did great!"

"That's good," Ken's mom replied.

"Deciding on the right engagement ring was an art all on its own. There were so many varied sizes, designs, and colours, that by the end of day one, my head was spinning. I didn't share too many details with Mimi though. She knew I was planning to propose at some point, but she did not know when or how I planned to do it."

"Any thoughts about the wedding yet or do you both want to enjoy being engaged for a while?" his mom asked cautiously.

"We haven't started talking about wedding plans yet, however, I am almost certain that there will be a ceremony in Nigeria,"

Ken said, a little hesitantly. He was not sure how his mother would respond to this latest information.

"That means grandbabies soon, right?" his mom replied.

Ken stood up and walked over to his mother. Then he gently took her hands in his. "How did we go from zero to one hundred mom? We only just got engaged."

His mother smirked.

"Bibi is coming over to meet the rest of the family for the first time and I want her to enjoy meeting everyone," Ken continued in a quiet but firm voice. "Please don't scare her off with baby talk."

His mother smiled and nodded. "I know, one step at a time. I just miss Jasmine and Ethan so much," she said, her voice shaking.

Ethan was Ken's five-year-old nephew, his older sister - Jasmine's son. There had been a big fallout between Jasmine and Mabel over some of Jasmine's lifestyle choices a couple of years ago. Since then, Jasmine had decided to stay away from her mom, which also meant that she stayed away from Ken. Ken had tried to reach her several times but had been unable to.

Before then, Ken's mom had been a constant presence in Ethan's life, looking after him three days a week while Jasmine worked. Now, Ken's mom would sometimes sit lost in thought for hours at a time holding Ethan's toy or clothing to her chest. Other times, she would move hurriedly towards the room she had set up for him saying he was awake and needed her. Ken missed his nephew too, but his heart bled for his mom more.

"Anyway, this weekend is all about you and Bibi, any plans at all?" Mabel asked as she dabbed at her tears.

"I want Bibi to see our hometown, my trophies, the schools I attended, and my teenage hangout spots. Seeing as you have decided to cook up a storm, I thought about inviting a few others for dinner tonight," Ken added.

"Well, I have invited your uncles, aunties, and a few friends. I hope you don't mind. I want to show off my son's beautiful fiancé, can you blame me? I am just so excited. I get to be the groom's mom and part of a wedding. I never got that with your sister because she decided to elope. Do you remember?"

Of course, he remembered. Like he could ever forget, even if he wanted to. His mom never failed to draw his attention to it whenever she could.

Ken decided not to dwell on that, and neither was he going to aid his mom.

"Do I have a choice mom? I already anticipated your plans and forewarned Bibi," Ken said, smiling. "You know we could have just gone out for a meal or ordered takeout."

"Not on my watch son, only the best for my daughter-in-law to be. I'm cooking everything from scratch."

Ken smiled.

"So, what are your plans for Bibi when she arrives?" his mother asked.

Ken looked at his mom, puzzled. He had just given her a list of what they would be doing. Was she as nervous as he was?

Then it dawned on him that his mom was appearing more forgetful of late and somewhat distracted. She would stop mid-sentence and seem to lose her train of thought. She also seemed a little withdrawn, he just thought it was because his dad's death anniversary was approaching. Should he be worried? Putting aside his niggles for now, he answered apprehensively.

"I will be picking her up at the train station this evening at about 4 p.m.," Ken said. "Then tomorrow, I'm going to show her our hometown, my trophies, the schools I attended, and my teenage hangout spots."

"Oh, I still have quite a bit to do before then. The guest room is not ready yet. Your aunty, Toni, will be arriving this afternoon to give me a hand," Mabel said.

Ken smiled. He knew his mom enjoyed entertaining and loved everything to be near perfect, if not perfect.

And it showed later that evening. Dinner was delicious, engaging, and fun. His mom and Aunty Toni really put forth their best. Everyone got along and had great conversations. Ken's godfather, Uncle Mark even invited everyone to hang out at his place the next day and then to church the morning after.

Bibi looked around the dinner table and smiled. These people would soon become her family. Something inside of her felt a slight sense of panic at the thought.

CHAPTER 3

"What have I done?"

Bibi felt panicked, dizzy, and nauseous at the same time. Closing her eyes for a few minutes, she willed the strange sensation to pass.

She had enjoyed a fantastic time with Ken and his family over the weekend. There had been a trip to the beach with Ken, dinner with his family, church service, lunches, and more.

Sighing deeply, Bibi rolled from her side onto her back and gazed vacantly at the ceiling. She just could not be bothered to get out of bed. She felt so low and quite miserable, yet she knew she should be elated.

Accepting his proposal was one thing but not having the temerity to tell her parents about Ken, let alone the proposal, was another thing.

Ken had called her the previous night, but she had feigned a headache because she was racked with so much guilt. She knew he was still reeling from the success of the weekend; she could hear it in his voice. She felt like an absolute betrayal right now.

Her head ached dully, and her eyes felt heavy as the weekend kept replaying over and over in her head. She loved thinking about their time together, but on the other hand, she could not help but think of how she was letting Ken down. She felt torn.

And now, she was wishing that the weekend had not yet happened. She wanted to turn back the hands of time. It was all happening too fast.

She just needed a bit more time to get her thoughts together before finding a way to tell her parents. Well, her mom. Her mom was the main one to convince.

Bibi reached for her phone. Maybe if she concentrated on her prayer and devotion for the day, she would feel better. She opened her bible and notepad app and tried to read the scripture, but the glare from her screen only made her headache worse. Suddenly, her grandmother's voice echoed in her head: *"When did your phone become your bible..., Abisola? There is depth and power in turning the pages of a book, particularly your bible."*

Her grandmother could never understand the fad of using a smartphone for virtually everything, even though Bibi's parents made sure to upgrade her phone regularly. Her phones were always as good as new, barely used.

Bibi read the same line multiple times and then gave up. Accepting defeat, she closed her eyes, but she could not un-hear her grandmother's voice. Her words echoed all around her. They were alive and loud. "Let God's promises shine on your problems!" she heard her grandmother say.

To drown out her grandmother's voice, Bibi started to hum one of her favourite songs by Tash Layton. As she came to the chorus, *"it's gonna be okay, it's gonna be okay, I 'm gonna be okay",* she felt better.

Feeling somewhat comforted, she allowed herself to drift into another subdued, restless slumber.

She was jolted out of her sleep by her ringing mobile phone after what seemed like hours but was mere minutes. Bibi ignored the ringing phone, but the caller was persistent. She already knew who it was and that there was no escaping it, however, she also was not going to cave, not right now anyway. Her mom would have to wait at least another hour or so. Right now, what she needed was a shower and caffeine to get her through the day, or at least get her through the conversation with her mother. She dragged herself out of bed then stepped into the shower and she just let the water flow over her head down to her toes. The ridiculously hot water should have scalded her, but instead, it felt so good and revitalising, it brought tears to her eyes again. She let the tears flow freely this time.

Perhaps because she needed an outlet.

Surprisingly, it felt like a good release, equally soothing.

* * *

"Bibi, my daughter, how are you doing?" her mother asked her when Bibi finally called her back.

"I am doing well, mommy. How about you?"

"You have finally finished your final exams, the latest baby lawyer in town! Bibi, you have done well." Her mother replied, ignoring Bibi's greeting, and just going right to the point of her call. There was a pause, then her mom's voice came back with such intensity,

"Iya Musa's second daughter is pregnant, can you imagine?"

"Mommy! Hauwa is in her final year at the university, pregnancy is not a dreadful thing."

"It is dreadful! Disgraceful too! What will people say in church and at the women's association? Her mom won't be able to walk around with pride, unlike me, I can walk around with my head and shoulders held high."

"Mom, it is not a competition." Bibi shrieked.

"My daughter, it is!!! Do you know anyone in our lineage that did not have at least two degrees before marriage?"

"Well, Maya too decided to get married immediately after her first degree and she is happily married," Bibi replied. Maya was her Aunty Joyce's daughter. She and Bibi had grown up together and were more like sisters.

"Bibi, Maya got married and did not fall pregnant in school, there is a difference. Although, her parents should have refused and told her to pursue a post-graduate course before marriage. I still cannot understand why she was in such a hurry to get married."

Within that same breath, her mom continued. "Two degrees already at your age, I am proud of you. We will be doing thanksgiving in church this Sunday." Her mother went on and on.

"Mommy, thanksgiving? What is the rush now? I am still waiting for my exam results, and I still need to defend my final dissertation. Be patient," Bibi said forcefully. It was the only language her mother understood. She could never understand her mother's need to make everything into a competition.

"Anyway, is Aunty Joyce still coming with you to my graduation?" Bibi asked, rolling her eyes, and deliberately changed the subject.

This whole conversation was killing her, and her headache had just intensified.

"Yes," her mother replied. She seemed to have gotten the message that Bibi did not want to talk about what was going on in everybody else's life. "Your Aunty Joyce and I will be coming for your graduation. We are so proud of you!"

"Good. I am glad to hear that, Mommy."

Bibi asked her mom how her father was doing, and how things were going back home in Nigeria before rushing her mother off the phone.

"Mommy, I must get ready to meet my academic supervisor. I will call you later when I am done."

Her mother seemed a little hesitant to get off the phone, but school was particularly important to her. Bibi knew that and often used it as her quickest way to escape her mother's awkward phone conversations. They bid each other goodbye, and Bibi promised to call her mother back after her meeting, knowing it was a promise she did not plan to keep.

Chapter 4

Ken joined Bibi for lunch on the patio of their favourite restaurant. He looked charming in a short-sleeved polo shirt with the buttons undone, showing off parts of his tanned, chiselled torso. His damp, neatly cropped, wheat blonde hair, glistened from the shadows of the sun's rays lurking behind the clouds.

His posture was tense, and Bibi could sense that he was not happy that she had been avoiding him since the weekend at his mother's house. They ordered drinks and menus were set in front of them. Ken jumped right into the reason they were there.

"Why haven't you told your parents about us?"

Today was warmer than it had been the last few days in town. Bibi was dressed in a short-sleeved tee and a pair of Tom Ford jeans. Her hands were clasped together on top of the table as she twiddled her thumbs. She looked better than he had ever seen her, even though she also looked like she had not been getting very much sleep.

Ken reached his hand out across the table and took Bibi's hand in his. "You keep promising, but nothing has changed," he said to her.

Bibi heard the pain in his voice. She did share in his pain, and she wished she had the courage it took to make this right, but she was struggling. She freed her hands and patted his gently.

"You have brought so much happiness into my life, Bibi," Ken continued. "But I am at my breaking point right now. I know what I want, no doubt. I want to spend the rest of my life with you. The question is, what do you really want?"

Bibi looked at his hands. She could not even look him in his eyes. She knew she was wrong for putting him in this predicament, but she was dealing with greater forces here. All he knew was that he had easily introduced her to his mother and the rest of his family, who had all eagerly been accepting of her, and he was expecting the same ease from her.

"You know I love you," Bibi said quietly.

"Really? All we need is love right now?" It was hard not to let his dejection and frustration show.

Ken leaned against the chair with his head tilted back and closed eyes. It was all he could do right now to control his tongue and emotions.

He had tried to convince Bibi to let him meet her parents. They came to the UK to visit her quite often. He could have met them the last time they were here months ago, but she had kept putting it off. He had even mentioned to her that he wanted to ask for her dad's permission before proposing to her, but that didn't happen either. Everyone of Ken's family and friends had met Bibi. Not only had she met everyone, but he always introduced her as his queen. He loved showing her off. He always said she was created perfectly; God had dedicated enough time into making her perfect.

Bibi watched Ken from across the table as the waiter returned with their orders. She had no explanations, no more excuses, and her heart was breaking seeing him like this. Bibi stared at her plate of piping hot food after the waiter left, waiting for Ken to say something. He did not.

Instead, Ken pulled his chair back slightly and sat up straight. He stared sadly at Bibi and said, "Bibi, I do not doubt your love for me. One thing I know for sure is that your parents' opinion and approval mean a lot to you. That is not a bad thing, I respect that. However, we need to cross this bridge of meeting them first, then we will follow from there."

Ken paused briefly before continuing.

"Bibi, is there something I am missing here? What exactly is holding you back? Are you ashamed of me?"

Bibi's eyes flew open wide. How could he ever think that?

"Ken, I am not ashamed of you, you know that. I am just not ready for you to meet them. Besides, I am beginning to feel pressured."

She knew she was being defensive, but she had to be, if she was going to buy herself more time. Things were different where she came from. Marrying someone outside her parents' circle was one thing, but for him not to be from Nigeria was another issue.

She knew Ken adored her and worshipped the ground she walked on. Sometimes, she thought it was all a dream because having him seemed too good to be true.

"Pressured? You think I am pressuring you?" Ken grimaced and shook his head. "Then I am backing down now!"

Suddenly, they both seemed to be on opposite sides of the fence. Bibi was speechless, and Ken seemed shocked and blindsided.

"Am I not good enough for you? Or you just don't think I can fund the luxurious and affluent lifestyle you are accustomed to. Which one is it, Bibi?" he asked so sharply that Bibi flinched.

Ken went on. "And not ready yet, really? Is that the best you can come up with? After dating for almost a year, and with your graduation just a few weeks away, what happens when you travel back home with your parents?"

Bibi did not respond. She was trying hard to think of something to say, but words were failing her now.

"I am beginning to doubt that you were ever as committed as I've been," Ken continued his tirade. "Maybe this was all fun for you while it lasted. Who knows, there is probably a rich lad waiting for you in Nigeria as we're sitting here having this silly conversation."

Tears began to fall down Bibi's face. She knew he was hurting, but so was she. She wished she could properly explain things to him, but she knew he would not understand. She reached out and placed her hand over his, but he quickly withdrew his hand.

"Bibi don't," he whispered shakily. "This is all over until I meet your parents, or at least, you tell them about us. There is no us for now."

With that, Ken got up in a fit of pique, walked over to the bar, and asked for a straight shot of brandy. After he had downed it in one go, he settled the bill and walked out of the restaurant without so much as a glance at Bibi, who sat wiping the tears from her eyes with the restaurant napkin.

This was their first major tiff; it could perhaps also be their last. Realizing that he had just broken up with her, Bibi felt a dull ache in her heart. She was not sure which hurt more, the fact that he had walked out on her or that he had broken up with her. She watched him as he walked out of the restaurant and wondered why she had not gone after him. Was she really that self-obsessed?

CHAPTER 5

Bibi walked slowly and deliberately, holding her Jimmy Choo embellished, high-heeled strappy sandals in her hands. Ken would have laughed at her while offering to hold them for her. She missed that already.

"Bibi, why did you even wear these in the first place?" he would have teased.

"Since it is lunch, I decided to go all out," she would have replied, laughing. She chuckled softly as these thoughts ran through her mind. Then suddenly, she felt the sting of tears behind her eyelids.

Bibi knew he was hurt; he barely drank. She knew she should have gone after him, and she wanted to, but the thought of telling her parents about him scared her more.

Yes, she was an adult in love with the man of her dreams, she knew what she wanted, but it just was not that straightforward.

She looked around. The restaurant where she and Ken had just broken up was situated right in the town centre. The town centre was quieter now, but it was usually quite busy at the weekends. Her apartment was only a short walk from the restaurant, so she and Ken would usually stroll there, hand in hand. This was where they came to either get breakfast, lunch, or dinner. Sometimes it was just to window shop or grab a quick cup of coffee. It was their thing to do together at least once over the weekend. It had become their ritual and they enjoyed every moment of it.

Weekends were their sacred time together and Bibi looked forward to that time together with Ken. They spent the time talking for ages about everything and nothing. Ken would whisper "I love you to the moon and beyond," in her ears, countless times. She would giggle every time he did that, she could never get enough of those words.

Sometimes, over countless weekends spent together, Bibi and Ken would fall into companionable silence and still feel connected; for Bibi, it could be catching up on schoolwork or watching Netflix. For Ken, it could be updating his music blog where he posted tracks from his favourite artistes and inspirations or scoring comprehension worksheets for the students in his English as a second language online class.

Bibi was still entranced by their memories together when she heard the voices of women yelling. She was not sure if they were yelling at each other or someone else. Bibi quickened her steps and rounded the corner where she saw two girls shouting drunkenly at a man standing at the door. It looked like they were being refused entry into the bar and were ticked off. The doorman was unfazed, he simply stood there like a statue, barely moving, even as the girls hit him repeatedly on his chest. The scene was quite hilarious. He was so big, and they were so small, they looked like ants trying to get onto an elephant. Okay, that was an exaggeration for effect. The sight made her chuckle, this would have made a good laugh for her and Ken.

As she approached her apartment's car park, she hoped Ken's car would still be there, that he had waited for her, so they could talk things through. Maybe he was even waiting for her upstairs. But she knew deep in her heart, that he was not.

Bibi's heart fell, and the tears began to fall again. She briefly contemplated going over to his house but decided against that. Ken was right, and she just did not have the answers he wanted right now.

Letting herself into her building and walking into the elevator, she let the tears flow freely, an older lady in the elevator looked at her curiously but quickly looked away. She looked vaguely familiar, and Bibi thought she may have seen her around.

To her astonishment, when the elevator stopped on the third floor and the lady hobbled out using her walking cane, she smiled at Bibi.

"Young lady, it's okay to cry, the sky does it too."

Bibi opened her mouth to respond but before she could think of a response, the doors shut.

Exiting the elevator on the fifth floor, she walked slowly down the L-shaped corridor to her door. Bracing herself, she unlocked the door to let herself into her empty apartment. It usually felt full of life on days like today. Yet, it felt empty and silent. They were not living together, but his things used to be everywhere, and she had always found that comforting. Now, the absence of his things quickened her heart with pain. His acoustic guitar, which had become a permanent fixture in her room, was now gone. And so was his "just in case" coat, scarf, and hat that once hung on the rack by the door. Tentatively, she walked to her bedroom, dreading what she might find missing. Over in the corner, where her study table stood, his bible and daily devotional book were gone. Bibi's legs gave way and she slid to the floor. Propping up herself by the foot of her bed, she glanced into thin air. He was truly gone. Ken was gone, and he had left a huge void!

She reached for her gold Ted Baker clutch bag that Ken had bought her for her last birthday and searched for her phone. She held on to her phone for a few minutes before dialling his number. She got his voicemail right away. "*You have just missed me, do your thing.*"

How she loved the sound of his voice. Putting her phone in front of her face, she stared at it, willing it to ring. It did not. After what seemed like an eternity she got up, got straight into bed fully clothed, and wept her heart out.

After she had cried to her heart's content, Bibi laid on her back and stared at the ceiling. She knew without any doubt, that her grandma would have accepted her and Ken as a couple, no questions asked. She smiled, closed her eyes, and quieted her mind so she could hear her grandmother's voice.

"*As long as he is God-fearing, kind, and has your interest at heart, then you will both be fine,*" she would have said. "*But make no mistake, marriage is no walk in the park. You must put one another first and God at the centre. That is all that matters to make it work.*"

Sad at the thought that her grandma would never get to meet Ken, Bibi felt a stream of fresh tears flowing down her cheeks.

If Aunty Joyce weren't so preoccupied with her husband's strange ailment, Bibi knew she would have been able to confide in her and maybe convince her to plant the seeds of her relationship with Ken in her mom.

"I can't burden her right now; she is already dealing with so much."

Aunty Joyce had always been a part of Bibi's life for as long as she could remember. Aunty Joyce's mother had died during childbirth, and her father had been so grief-stricken, that he had been unable to care for her as a baby. Bibi's grandmother, who was a distant relative to Aunty Joyce, had taken her in and raised her.

When Bibi's grandmother took Aunty Joyce in, Bibi's mother was herself only six months old, so they were raised together as sisters. They did everything together growing up and were remarkably close. Aunty Joyce's daughter, Maya, and Bibi were also born six months apart, and, although they grew up in separate homes, were also close. They lived not too far away from each other growing up and even attended the same schools.

When Maya was getting married, Bibi pretty much moved into Maya's parents' house the few weeks leading up to the ceremony. She and Maya had planned the wedding together, down to every little detail. During that time, Maya had also confided in Bibi, telling her she had noticed a personality change in her dad.

Uncle Joe, once a boisterous, energetic man, was now forgetful and withdrawn. Maya simply could not understand what was happening to him. He would forget what he had eaten for breakfast and seemed uninterested in her wedding plans. He could not even remember the name of her fiancé.

But when Maya tried to discuss this with her mother, Aunty Joyce was dismissive of her concerns. Eventually, Uncle Joe was taken to the hospital, but even then, Aunty Joyce still refused to discuss the details with Maya. She only overheard parts of the conversation her mom was having on the phone.

"People are saying it is part of ageing, but he is only in his fifties, and I don't know anyone else who is this forgetful," her mother would often say.

"He has completely lost interest in everything. He stops abruptly during conversations, looking lost, and he is quite irritable these days," Maya would hear her mother say to the doctor who was reassuring to her that all was being done to make sure that he was okay.

Sadly, he never was okay. Instead, he steadily got worse.

For Maya's traditional wedding ceremony, two days before the church wedding, her mother and other elders in the family decided it would be best if her father did not take part in the festivities because of his "ageing process."

Instead, he was kept in a room with a distant relative watching over him, so he would not wander into the main compound where the ceremony was being held.

Maya tried to speak to her mom, but the response was always, "If your husband's people should see that side of your father, they may decide not to ask for your hand in marriage anymore."

"But Emeka is not like that; he will understand, and I am not ashamed of Dad."

"Well, the doctor has said it is ageing and probably depression, which is a stigma."

"Mom, depression is not a stigma, it is real."

"Maya, you are not old enough to be having this conversation, this concerns the elders and his brothers, just concentrate on getting married."

Maya knew how important her wedding was to her father, especially the traditional wedding. This was usually an important part of a wedding for parents. It meant the groom, his family members, and friends, coming with gifts to formally ask for her hand in marriage.

She had been looking forward to this day and had always expected kneeling in front of her dad, his chest puffed out with such ego and pride as he blessed her. Only, it was never to be, one of her uncles blessed her instead, and not even one of the ones she held in high regard. This uncle was secretly nicknamed 'extra mouth' by herself and Bibi because he always only ever magically appeared at mealtimes and mostly spoke with his mouth full of food, then would pick his teeth noisily afterwards.

From stories she had heard, he had also kicked against her dad marrying her mom years ago. He did not like her mom and only tolerated her because of the gifts he got from her.

Later in the evening, whilst changing into another outfit, Bibi tried to console Maya as she cried uncontrollably, lamenting over and over, "I am old enough to get married but not old enough to get involved in my dad's health matters, how ironic?"

It hurt Bibi so much that on what should have been one of the happiest days of Maya's life, she was lamenting over her father's absence at her marriage ceremony. She had seen Maya go through the motions of getting married, her body present but her mind absent.

She looked tired; Bibi had to keep reminding her to smile. "You don't want to look through your wedding album in the future with regrets," Bibi kept telling Maya.

"Well, who cares? Dad is not going to be in the album anyway."

Her dad did not get to walk her down the aisle too.

At the reception party, one of their distant relatives whispered into her ears, "we know you are pregnant, just get through today, and then you can rest." If Maya were in her true form, there would have been a sassy comeback for this busybody aunty, but at that moment, she just could not be bothered.

Still staring at the ceiling, Bibi closed her eyes and tried to fall asleep, but sleep eluded her. She checked her phone one last time. Nothing!

Bibi abandoned her bed, headed to the living room, and turned on the television. She had forgotten to check the time; because if she had, she would have realised that her and Ken's favourite show was on. Smiling through the tears, Bibi, pulled the throw from the back of the sofa, wrapped herself tightly in it, and curled up to watch their show. She laughed and cried, laughed, and cried, until she dozed off to the fading voices in the background.

Chapter 6

Ken woke up the next day and realised that he missed his father now more than ever before. His parents' marriage had been a loving one. His father dotted on his mother and treated her like a queen. He would open doors for her, buy her flowers, and they even held hands often. Ken envied his parents' marriage now. He knew they had endured their share of challenges, but they always dealt with it. His father believed that a "happy wife made a happy life."

To his father, his mother completed him. Because of what he had seen of his parents' marriage, Ken had always hoped to find a woman to match him the way his mother had matched his father. He thought he had found the right woman, only to find that the right woman was not even ready to be his wife. Had he read the signs wrong?

Sadly, his father had died suddenly of a heart attack over ten years ago. His death had been unexpected since he had led a completely healthy and simple lifestyle. After his father's death, Ken was so angry, he kept asking God why. He was not sure if that was the reason, he chose missionary work after dental school; to feel close to his dad or because it was his calling. Right now, he was beginning to question most of his decisions again.

Hoping to get an explanation for his father's premature death, Ken threw himself hungrily into the scriptures. It was as if his life depended on it. For years, he did not allow himself to grieve but instead held on to his feelings. His mother, on the other hand, was so accepting of his death, even though she was completely heartbroken over her loss.

And now, Ken was missing him more than ever. His father would have prayed with him, counselled him wisely, telling him to go to church, speak, and listen to God. His uncle, Mark, who was also his godfather, had stepped in and served as a father figure after his father died. Uncle Mark, completely dependable when it came to men matters and matters of the heart, but Ken just wanted his dad to be a part of his happiness even if it was short-lived.

* * *

The last couple of days had been absolutely agonising. Not having any contact with Bibi had probably been one the most difficult things he had ever had to do. He missed her with every fibre of his being, but he also knew that this was the appropriate thing to do right now. He had been struggling particularly with the fact that he had proposed to Bibi without her dad's blessings, but he kept hoping that the proposal would propel his introduction to them. Why would she not introduce him to her parents? It had all been such a mystery!

She knew of his background in ministry. He was comfortable around people from other races. In fact, when he and Bibi started dating, Ken started worshipping at her church and hardly felt out of place, even though West Africans predominately attended the church. And she knew that was because he had spent parts of his childhood in Gambia, Ghana, and Sierra Leone. His father had worked as a missionary surgeon before retiring back to the UK. Ken enjoyed the vibe and extroverted way of worship at Bibi's church so much that he had invited his friend, Jay, to worship with them one Sunday and he had never left. Jay described the worship as over the top and a bit much but still came with Ken most Sundays.

He loved everything about her, her full name *A - bi - sola: Born into a wealthy family*. Her name completely embodied everything about her and her striking features. From her full, straight, and silky jet-black hair, which she usually wore in a pony-tail, to her striking facial features, to her slender, dainty waist, to her hourglass shape, to her light brown even skin tone and her heavenly voice.

God must have created her on a Sunday because she is utterly perfect. He certainly dedicated enough time to moulding her.

He missed the coconut smell of her hair and the way the tendrils that escaped from her ponytail danced around her face in the breeze.

When he closed his eyes with a deep sigh and allowed himself think of choir practice, he pictured them together, making music to worship the one and only true God. Ken played the guitar and sang; Bibi played the keyboard and sang too. Depending on their various schedules, meeting at church, or going together every Friday evening for choir practice, was something he looked forward to. During practice, Ken and Bibi's eyes would continuously meet. And she would play coy by smiling and looking away shyly.

Cutting off contact with Bibi hurt so much that life itself had lost its colour. But she had left him no other choice. He had prayed and pondered his decision for weeks. The answer had not been an easy one, but it had been the only one he could come up with that made sense. Moving over to the sofa, Ken grabbed the remote control, turned on the television to find his and Bibi's favourite show was on. He wondered what she must be doing at that very moment.

Sitting deeper into the sofa, he crossed his legs and settled down for a night of laughter and sadness without Bibi.

CHAPTER 7

Bibi shuddered at the thought of experiencing grief again. The heartache and pain she felt were unbearable. She felt drained and was barely functioning. She just wanted the nightmare to be over.

Ken would know how to make her feel better, his smile alone could melt away her aches and send tingles down her spine and through her toes. He just knew how to make her feel better, he always said the right things, and sometimes he knew when to just hold her, no words needed.

Shortly after Bibi met Ken, she had lost her grandmother back in Nigeria. Ken at once recognised her grief and supported her throughout her grieving period, with no expectations or judgements.

All Bibi did was cry for the first few days after her parents told her about the news over the phone. Initially, she was in shock, so all she could do was curl up in bed and eventually fall asleep. She later woke up and realised that her grandmother was truly gone, it wasn't just a bad dream. It was then that she got so angry that she hadn't had the chance to say goodbye. The pain was unbearable, she could not eat or sleep, and nothing made sense anymore.

For a little while, her studies suffered as her zeal waned and all she wanted to do was sleep.

Her grandmother had lived with Bibi's family for as long as she could remember. During school holidays, she wasn't allowed out as much except to go to Maya's house and church, so she ended up spending a lot of time together with her grandmother and sometimes Maya, when Maya stayed over, especially when her parents travelled out of the country.

She remembered her grandmother's stories about her own childhood and what it was like growing up in rural Nigeria. Her favourite memory was the story of how her grandmother had met her grandfather, and how her grandmother spoke so highly of him, and with so much love in her voice, even though he had died long before Bibi was born.

Ken was her rock through it all.

And Bibi was grateful for his support because it got her through one of the grimmest times in her life. She had been close to her grandmother, so the sense of loss was profound. Ken understood this pain very well, having lost his own father years earlier.

Bibi sat up in bed and looked at the bedside clock; she had about three more hours before she had to leave for church. She headed to the kitchen to boil a kettle of water for tea. Then she sat at the small, rectangular dining table, which sometimes doubled as her study table, and thought about her grandmother some more.

Her grandmother had been her confidant. She would often tell her grandma about her dreams of becoming a famous singer. She even shared her experiences with Adeniyi, her ex-boyfriend. She told her grandmother how sad she had been when she and Adeniyi broke up. It was her grandmother and Maya who saw her through that breakup. Bibi was grateful to have them during that time because she needed them. Adeniyi was her first love, the man she thought she would marry, so the loss of their relationship was devastating for Bibi.

She met Adeniyi whilst studying for her first degree in Nigeria, but she never introduced him to her parents. In fact, she only saw him during holidays under the pretext of going to see Maya or going to choir practice.

Born to well-educated and affluent Nigerian parents, it was expected that Bibi would follow in their footsteps by either becoming a lawyer or engineer. Perhaps, even a doctor. Her father ran a big, reputable construction company in Lagos, and her mother ran one of the city's largest law firms. But Bibi wanted to sing. She had always done well at school and scored highly but what she loved to do most of all was sing. She had sung at church from an early age, and all through high school, she had always hoped to make a career out of it but deep down she knew her parents would never entertain the idea.

So, she chose law. Adeniyi was understanding at first and thought it was sweet, but by their final year, he struggled to understand why he could not visit her at home, and it began to put a lot of strain on their relationship. Eventually, they broke up. It was for the best anyway because unlike Maya who knew she was ready to marry Emeka straight out of university, Bibi was hesitant. Adeniyi said he was ready to get married shortly after graduation. She knew that her parents would frown upon the idea. They had already planned for her to travel to the UK for her postgraduate study after her call to the bar. Adeniyi knew she had to go to law school, and he was prepared to support her through that, except he wanted them to get married first. He already had a job lined up at his dad's reputable financial institution. He always said he was willing to financially support her studies after they got married.

Maya had married young, but to the man she loved. And her parents had supported her decision all the way through. Maya seemed happy with her life's choices. She was happy being at home as a full-time wife and mom, despite completing a degree in communication and language art. It made Bibi a little envious of Maya.

The kettle began to whistle. Bibi grabbed a mug from the kitchen cupboard, placed a tea bag in it, and poured piping hot water over the tea bag. Then she let it sit for a bit so that the tea bag could bleed into the water. While she waited, Bibi continued to recall her time spent with Ken after the death of her grandmother.

That period had been a defining moment for them; Ken had been there for her and did not take advantage of her in any way. He gently encouraged her to see her general practitioner, but she refused because she did not see the need. She did not feel feverish or unwell, why would she be going to see her doctor?

But Ken was relentless as he explained that while he thought she was experiencing grief, it was important for her to be sure that she was not sinking into depression as well.

After several weeks of insomnia, restlessness, and extreme sadness, she finally gave in and went to see her general practitioner. She was especially worried that she was quickly losing weight. Her general practitioner prescribed her short-term night sedatives that helped her to sleep. That made her feel better.

With Ken's unwavering support, she started to smile again, even started to sing in the shower too. He bought her favourite meals and even tried to cook once or twice. There was one hilarious moment when he tried to make *eba* and *draw* soup. It was not too bad, and the fact that he had tried meant a great deal to her. He also remembered to play the movies that she loved which made her laugh.

Remembering Maya's reaction when she told her about her visit to see her doctor, because of her grief, made her chuckle as she took her first sip of tea. Maya had laughed so hard and asked if there was a specific medication one could take to overcome grief.

"All this 'white way' of thinking, Bibi. Which one is talking to the doctor again when someone dies? Is it not to cry, be sad, and then get on with life? Anyway, you are gradually beginning to think like them. Is this Ken rubbing off on you or has it just been there? I miss you anyway, it was hard losing grandma. To think you could not attend the funeral service. I wish you were around for us to have consoled one another but it is well," Maya had said to Bibi on the phone.

"Maya, grief is real and there is certainly more than one way to grieve. It is not as straightforward as you describe it. I realised that grief is not linear, nor does it affect two people the same way. For some, it could be repressed for a while. For others, it could manifest almost immediately. It sometimes felt like I was free-falling through a bottomless dark hole. Ken was my constant through that bleak period, he pulled me back from despair."

"So, he's a good guy, eh?" Maya simply said.

"Of course, he is," Bibi replied.

"Then why are you hiding him? Why are you hiding a good guy from your parents?"

Bibi did not respond then and probably could not respond now if asked this question again. But she knew that Maya had asked the right question. Why was she hiding Ken from her parents if she could so easily agree with Maya that he was indeed a good guy?

CHAPTER 8

Bibi sipped the last drop of tea from her cup and nibbled on the piece of peanut butter toast she had since made to go with her cup of tea. She and Ken's favourite podcast was playing on her phone, but she was not as focused on it as she normally was when they listened to it together.

The podcast called 'the naked marriage,' being broadcast by a well – known couple, Dave, and Ashley Willis. She and Ken considered Dave and Ashely Willis their model couple – Christians, enthusiastic followers of Christ, married for about 20 years, and still madly in love with each other.

Bibi allowed her mind to wander to the morning she had ahead of her. She felt a slight excitement as she looked forward to seeing Ken at church. She hoped to get a chance to talk to him, especially since they had not spoken to or seen one another since he broke things off with her. She had skipped choir practise on Friday to focus on her dissertation and rounding things up at school hence she had not been to church the last two Sundays.

She looked at the time and realised she had to get ready to leave the house. Bibi dropped the crust of her toast on her plate, rubbed hands together to get rid of the crumbs, then sent a text message to Naomi to confirm that she would be meeting her downstairs as planned. She needed Naomi there as her wingman because she could not face Ken alone. She was feeling rather fragile and needed moral support.

Pulling her robe tighter around her, Bibi stood up, walked to the French windows, and looked out at the sea of umbrellas. It had rained all night but was drizzling now. She watched as people hurried by, some in their Sunday bests going to church, others in a rush to get to work or on their way home from their night shifts. Feeling a deep yearning for Ken, she decided it was time to get ready. She needed to look her best for Ken.

Forty minutes after entering the bathroom, Bibi was finally ready. As she brushed out the last of the tangled locks from her hair, she caught the reflection of her engagement ring in the mirror.

"Should I still be wearing this?" She asked herself for the first time since the breakup. She had barely thought about having the ring on her finger. Sighing deeply, she eased the ring off her finger and set it down on top of the dresser. Their engagement was not even public yet. What if people should start to ask questions or even congratulate her?

Bibi smoothed her dress and took one last glance at herself in the mirror. Just then, her phone chimed. It was Naomi texting to let her know that she was outside. Gathering her umbrella, phone, bible, and handbag, Bibi headed out of her apartment and towards Naomi's yellow mini cooper. As she lowered herself into the car, and collapsed her umbrella, the rain suddenly stopped. Then the sun shone brightly through the grey clouds. Bibi smiled for the first time since waking up as she thought *"this is a good omen."*

"Hi girl," Bibi said, settling into the passenger seat.

"Hey, so you ready?" Naomi asked, as she reversed the car out of the parking spot and headed for the exit of Bibi's apartment building.

"I think I am," Bibi said, clicking on her seatbelt. She was nervous, she could admit that. She was not sure where she stood with Ken. The two of them had not spoken since he had stormed out of the restaurant, and he had been ignoring her calls. She was just hoping that he would at least be amenable to speaking with her in the Lord's house.

Naomi pulled into the church parking lot about twenty minutes later. Bibi did a quick subtle sweep of the parking lot and was disappointed when she did not see Ken's car. She hoped he was simply running late or perhaps he came in with Jay as she caught a glimpse of Jay's car. But he was not with Jay. She found that out when she and Naomi walked up to the church and came across Jay, who was also on his way up the stairs to the prayer room where church workers usually met before service. Jay worked with the media and communications department.

"Hey, Bibi, how are you doing and where is Ken? It has been ages since I saw you two," he said with a big grin.

Immediately, her stomach was in knots.

Bibi wondered if Jay knew about their engagement and later events but nothing in his whole demeanour suggested that he knew anything. Mumbling an answer under her breath, she quickly tagged along with Mildred, an assistant pastor, who happened to walk by. She pretended she had to catch up on something urgent.

"Oh, hi Bibi, can I help you with anything?" Pastor Mildred asked without stopping but turning her head slightly in the direction of Bibi.

"Nothing that can't wait, I can see you are in a hurry right now." Before the response came, Bibi ducked into the restroom nearby.

Holding onto a wash hand basin to steady herself, she let out a deep sigh and rued the moment she let him walk away from her. She should have stopped him. Closing her eyes tight to stop the tears that threatened to fall from under her eyelids, she heard her mom's words in her head.

"Always behave like a duck – keep calm and unruffled on the surface but paddle vigorously underneath."

Pulling herself together she squared her shoulders up high, head straight and just as she tried to open the door, Ayo rushed through almost knocking Bibi over.

This morning could not get any worse. Bibi smiled weakly at Ayo, who stared at her suspiciously.

"Hi Bibi, haven't seen you in a while. How are you?" Ayo said through her forced smile and cold gaze.

Bibi tried so hard not to roll her eyes. She and Ayo had never cared much for one another. She despised Bibi and had been clear about her feelings the moment she learnt of her relationship with Ken.

She still could not believe Ayo had felt entitled to her opinion when she callously told Bibi, "So clearly none of our single brothers is good enough for you that you have felt the need to bring someone who is an outsider in here as your boyfriend."

Bibi had been so shocked at the time that her mouth gaped open in disbelief. They both sang in the choir and tolerated one another. They were always polite and distant, never friends.

Bibi was thankful for the fact that she would not be singing today, normally with Ken around, she could not care less about anyone; the side looks or comments; but today, she knew that her voice and non-verbal cues would certainly betray her. They both decided earlier on in their relationship, to enjoy what they shared rather than tire themselves in defending their relationship.

Shrugging her shoulders, Bibi gave a monosyllabic answer, then exited the restroom swiftly. She was here today for one purpose and one purpose only. She made her way to the main sanctuary, hoping Ken would have arrived by now.

She scanned the congregation and her eyes met Naomi's. Naomi beckoned her over to sit in an empty chair she had reserved next to her.

"Everything okay?" Naomi whispered to her as she settled into her seat. Bibi did not trust herself to speak, all she did was nod while looking around yet again expectantly.

No Ken. Disappointment washed over her.

* * *

During the praise and worship rendition, her spirits soared because she felt the lyrics speak to her body, soul, and spirit. The upbeat songs got her moving, smiling, and singing from her heart. Toward the end of worship, the songs moved to a more sombre note and her mind shifted to Ken, as he usually played a big part here. Rounding up worship.

The service began, and Bibi tried to concentrate on the pastor's words. Her mind kept wandering and she had to keep stopping herself from crying. She just went with the motions. It is obvious as day that he did not want to risk bumping into her. Refusing to take her calls, not being at church...it was all so much clearer now. He was serious about not being with her if she was unwilling to do the right thing.

At various times during the sermon, Naomi would touch her lightly on her arm and back. There were no words, yet she felt comforted.

As soon as the service ended, she was straight out the main door, she could not bring herself to hang around to exchange pleasantries.

Jay had tried to accost her and Naomi, but she had brushed through like she did not see him. Burying her head in her bag, she pretended to be searching for something.

Bibi must have been in a trance as she plodded straight past Naomi's car to the bus stop right ahead. She stepped onto the bus standing with its doors open, without knowing the bus number nor its intended direction. She must have looked pitiful, or the bus driver must have been in a happy mood, as he waved her on when she was fumbling through her bag for loose change.

She knew Naomi would be furious but right now, she just needed space to think. Making her way to the back of the bus, she settled by the window, sent a quick message to Naomi. Then she switched her phone off.

Riding on the bus for what seemed like an eternity, the feeling of weariness and loneliness suddenly overcame her, and she started to tremble. Looking down at her legs, she realised they were bare. She had no tights on. No coat or any other layer. All she had on was her Misa Los Angeles chiffon knee-length dress. She felt cold. This was a bad idea.

Feeling dejected, she pulled the bell to disembark at the next stop. As she descended the stairs, she nodded her gratitude to the bus driver. After the bus pulled away, she stood at the bus stop for a little while before walking down the road till she came to a cafe. She hesitated briefly before pushing her way through the double set of doors. Then she settled at a table around the back and waited for a waiter to approach. She switched her phone back on and just as she had expected, numerous chimes came flooding through. Letting out an exasperated sigh, she texted Naomi asking for a ride home. She did not even know where she was.

A quick glance at the bottom of the takeaway menu told her what she needed to know. She texted the address to Naomi who responded right back. Then she sipped on the hot drink she had ordered and waited patiently for Naomi to arrive.

When Naomi turned up to get her, there were no questions and no reprimands. Just a reassuring smile and a big bear hug.

"Thank you for trusting me, I am always here for you Bibi," Naomi said after pulling away gently from her while still holding her.

Naomi removed her cotton scarf from the loop around her neck, shook it to full length, and wrapped it around Bibi before gently leading her to the car park round the back.

Bibi loved that Naomi left her to her thoughts as she drove her home. They made a brief stop at her local Thai restaurant where Naomi picked up the food she had ordered. Naomi rushed in and out of the restaurant with a bag which she placed behind Bibi's seat.

As the fragrant smell filled the car, Bibi's stomach growled with hunger.

CHAPTER 9

Ken re-read the email a second time as he rubbed his temples. He had a missionary trip to Uganda coming up in two weeks and the email was a "gentle reminder." He had less than 72 hours to accept or decline the invitation. And for the first time, he was unsure of which choice to pick. He had never declined in the past.

Later that night, he tossed and turned for hours, and, in the wee hours of the morning, he decided to go for a run. Running normally relaxed his nerves, but his mind was being pulled in so many different directions. He had been on edge a lot lately. It had been several weeks since his breakup with Bibi, plus now he had this deadline he was utterly torn about.

This was something he could have easily discussed with Bibi, but now that there was no Bibi, he had to make this decision on his own. Bibi had tried to reach him on several occasions, but he had not taken any of her calls because from her text messages and voice messages, he knew she still had not told her parents about him, which should make going to Uganda a no-brainer, but the last week had brought with it, its own issues.

He ended his five-mile run with a shower and quickly fell asleep as soon as his head hit his pillow.

The next day, he met his mother for lunch. He had not seen her much since she seemed busier these days. She was in and out of the hospital for various medical tests due to symptoms she had been experiencing over the last 12 months. She had tried to keep it all quiet, but it was time for Ken to know what was going on.

Initially, Ken thought his mom was taking him out because he had been mopping around the house and she wanted to cheer him up. She had sprung on him at home unannounced the other day and found him looking quite the mess. She had spent hours helping him clean up his house. She had seemed quite upbeat and encouraging then. But sitting across from her now, he could tell that something was not right.

"What's wrong, mom?" he asked her.

"Oh, nothing, honey, nothing," she said, brushing him off.

Ken looked at his mother suspiciously. Something about her was different. He could not place his finger on it, but he had noticed her becoming a lot more absent-minded lately. This made him even more worried. He knew his mother and usually when she said he didn't need to worry about something, that's when he typically ended up worried about something.

It turns out that she had been unwell for a while and her friend, Shona, Naomi's mom, had been by her side the entire time.

"I am still waiting for a formal diagnosis. However, I have been having trouble finding the right words, and sometimes following conversations, my orientation and concentration seem off too."

Pausing for a while, she looked up and cocked her head to the side, and with so much sadness, she continued. "Shona also tells me I have become quite forgetful so not sure what we may be dealing with yet."

"Why didn't you tell me, mom? You know I would have been there for you if I had known you were sick," Ken said. He was trying not to let the hurt and anger show. Why would she keep him in the dark?"

Putting her hand over his, she gently reassured him that it was the way she wanted it and she had no intentions of stopping him from living his life. She was a retired nurse, so she shared her suspicions of what might be ailing her. She may have a case of younger onset dementia, but she was not sure. The tests would confirm. For now, all they could do was wait.

Ken felt a little panicked. Even if things turned out well with Bibi, there was no way he could move to Nigeria now with his mom's impending diagnosis. And Bibi had made it clear that she had no plans to live anywhere else, especially since she was planning to take over the running of her mom's chambers in the future. Things seemed so final at that moment and Ken felt sad, not only for his mother's deteriorating health but also for the slow death of his love story with Bibi.

∗ ∗ ∗

Ken and his mother left the restaurant after barely touching their meals. They walked in silence along a familiar path next to the car park, taking in the beautiful green scenery around them. Mabel loved the smell of grass, not surprising as she had grown up on a farm. Coming to a bench by the lake, she sat down and

patted the space next to her. Ken sat beside his mother looking so downcast, and her heart broke for him.

Mabel told Ken; she would have to put her affairs in order. He and Shona would be her lasting powers of attorney. As one of her lasting powers of attorney, Ken made her promise to call him as soon as she gets confirmation of the final diagnosis. She nodded and he knew that she needed him. His mom looked scared.

"I'm going to be here for you, Mom. Always. I will be right here for you."

His mother smiled weakly and simply laid her head on his shoulder.

Yes, now was not the right time to be going away, his mother needed him now. He was going to make a quick trip and come right back to be by his mom's side soon enough. This trip was just to tie up loose ends.

CHAPTER 10

Bibi's mother was on the phone sounding exasperated. "Bibi, I went to see Joyce and her husband last week. He had deteriorated. At first, Joyce said he was not at home but a while later, he came out with the maid running after him. The maid started begging Joyce, saying "madam I couldn't stop him, am so sorry ma." He looked so dishevelled, had lost weight, and looked like he had wet himself. He was muttering to himself; he did not even recognise me when I greeted him," Bibi's mother said, letting her concern spill through the phone.

"What did Aunty Joyce say, when Uncle Joe came out of the house like that?" Bibi asked.

"Joyce was speechless. For a minute or two, she just stood there, stared vacantly. Then she finally shouted at the girl to take him back inside and keep him there."

"That is so sad, mom. Aunty Joyce must have been really embarrassed."

"But she should not have been. I am practically her sister," her mom replied, sounding hurt.

"What is happening, mom, is he unwell?"

Her mother sighed heavily. "Bibi, I do not know. But we have been told not to tell anyone about it. Joyce has been talking to her pastor and he has asked her to continue to fast and pray.

Hopefully, he will get better soon. We are not sure where this strange affliction is coming from. Joyce was looking quite spent and tired too."

"Why did Aunty Joyce seek treatment elsewhere instead of Dr Gordon's hospital," Bibi asked. She often wondered why Aunty Joyce and Maya attended her dad's best friend's hospital but never Uncle Joe, well as far as she could remember.

"Well, that is a long story. Dr Gordon, Joe, and your dad were all close friends for years, until Dr Gordon and Joe had a big fall out. They have since managed to remain civil, but Joe swore never to step foot in his hospital." Bibi really wanted to ask more questions, but she knew her mom would shut her down.

"Anyway, back to the reason for my call," her mom continued, quickly switching topics. "I wanted to discuss one or two things with you about coming home after graduation, your dad and I will go into more detail when we see you, but I wanted to...."

"Mom?"

"Yes."

"Can I interrupt you?"

"Uh, what is it, Bibi?"

Bibi hesitated.

"What is it?" her mom pressed her.

"Well, I was thinking that instead of going back to Nigeria, with you and daddy after graduation as planned, can you ask daddy if I can stay back for a while longer? A couple of things are happening right now that I need to take care of before I leave."

"What exactly do you mean by that? I really do not think your dad will agree to that."

Her mom paused briefly before going on. "Is there a reason you are thinking of staying back? You seemed eager to come back after your first semester and now you are backtracking."

"Um......" Bibi started to speak.

"We have put quite an effort into planning your home coming, not to talk of money spent. Bisola, your dad just bought you a penthouse apartment, exclusively furnished. In fact, you will love it, a brand-new car is also waiting for you, with your own private chauffeur."

Bibi sighed deeply and placed the phone in speaker mode. Then she rested her head on her pillow and listened to her mother's voice in the background. This was all too much. She just wanted some peace. When was her mom going to learn that money was not the answer to everything?

"Your office is ready," her mother continued. "Moreover, your dad is organising a big welcome party for you. Dr Gordon and his family will be there too. His son, Dapo, has just moved back home after studying medicine in the States. You know he is a trained surgeon."

Her mother paused as if for effect. When she got no reaction from Bibi, she continued, her voice slightly raised this time.

"You ought to start thinking about marriage right now, you are not getting any younger. You have not introduced any man to us, so your dad thinks it is a clever idea for the both of you to meet."

Bibi sat up abruptly. "Mom, but I barely know Dapo. I do not even love him." Bibi rolled her eyes, something she would never dare to do in her mother's physical presence.

"What has love got to do with anything? He is from an incredibly good family, and they are influential and wealthy. Moreover, you met him enough times at family celebrations before he left the country."

"I must go now, mom. Greetings to everyone."

"Okay, my dear. But before I forget, Maya is heavily pregnant with her second child, so hurry up. Your biological clock is ticking."

Bibi shook her head. "Okay, mom I know. Maya and I speak regularly." Bibi hung up with a loud sigh, stood up, paced around several times before she leaned against the door. Having her parents accept Ken was important, especially with her being the only child. She knew this, their hopes were riding on her decisions and her future, and she was beginning to feel the pressure. She had promised Ken that she would tell her parents about their engagement before they arrived in the UK for her graduation. Yet, here she was, on the other side of the phone line, and she had chickened out again!

It made her angry just thinking about the fact that she was feeling pressured to marry a man she did not know. It made her angry that she could not tell them about Ken. And it made her even angrier that Ken had not been patient with her and was now nowhere to be found. He was not answering her calls, and she had not heard from him in almost a month.

Before now, her parents were always telling her to focus on her studies and not to get distracted by relationships. Now, within a few weeks of her completing her final exams, she was being confronted about not bringing a man home. The last time her parents visited her, just before her final semester began, she had timidly told her mom that she had a close male friend she wanted to bring round for dinner. What did her mom say?

"A male friend is not your priority right now, focus on your final semester," she had said sternly.

What if she had not met Ken? Did her parents think men were readily manufactured or produced somewhere for graduates? They had spewed the typical "concentrate on your studies," line and yet expected her to be ready for marriage upon graduating. Where was one supposed to meet their spouse, if not at school? They should know better! Afterall, they met in school as undergraduates too!

Suddenly, Bibi felt enraged and tired, she just wanted to lie down. Walking over to her bed, she collapsed onto it and repeatedly banged her phone on the soft mattress. When she was exhausted, she broke down and cried. The frustration of the last four weeks weighed heavily on her shoulders as her body heaved with sorrow. When she could cry no more, she curled up into a ball and fell asleep.

CHAPTER 11

"There is no need to get emotional, Mom," Ken said dolefully as she turned on the waterworks. He pretended to look for something in his backpack, so she did not see him welling up as well. They had arrived at the airport not too long ago, and Ken had just returned to his mother's side after checking in.

"I just can't help but worry that you may have been a bit hasty in making your decision," his mom blubbered.

"I need to do this for myself, I have thought long and hard about this bold step. Just know that I will be a phone call away and will be here as soon as you need me," Ken said, reassuring his mom.

Then he hugged her one last time before he turned to get his hand luggage.

"Kenneth!"

Ken stopped. He would always know that voice even in his deepest slumber. He certainly was not dreaming, it had to be real.

His mom looked at the caller and back at Ken with her mouth wide open, clearly perplexed. He dropped all that he was holding and held out his arms wide.

She flung herself into his arms. The feeling was pure delight, he was not letting go ever again. He had missed her so much. Their mom was so stunned that she could barely move even as she was pulled into the hug. Mabel kept touching her all over, just to be sure she was there in the flesh.

Jasmine! Jasmine!!!!

Then he saw it, that smile Ken had missed so much.

"Mom, mom," a small voice interrupted their hugging circle.

Mabel's eyes widened and her smile broadened, as she looked at the little boy holding on to Jasmine's leg.

Jasmine looked at her mom as she knelt beside the boy.

"Ethan, this is your grandma, remember? Remember her?"

Ethan nodded his head gently, causing Mabel to burst out in tears. He remembered her!

Jasmine gently encouraged Ethan to go to his grandma.

Mabel waited impatiently for the hug that was to follow, as Ethan walked towards her a little hesitantly. The hug was everything she had imagined it would be when she saw him again. It took her to heaven and back just thinking of this moment that was real. She was getting her second chance.

"Why don't I get a hug too," Ken chipped in. "I am your Uncle Ken, the coolest uncle ever!" They all laughed whilst Mabel gently let him go so that Ken could get a hug too.

Jasmine stood behind them crying. It was a bittersweet moment for all of them.

Ken momentarily forgot his own heartache and savoured the moment. Thankfully, he had enough time before he had to board his plane.

"Let's grab a table and a bite to eat," he said. He was not hungry, he just really wanted to enjoy this moment with his nephew, sister, and his mom, for as long as he could.

His mom nodded and reached out her hand to Ethan, who willingly took it this time. She gripped his little hand firmly like she was afraid of losing him again.

Minutes later, the four of them were seated at a corner table inside a small restaurant not too far from the security checkpoint at the airport. After placing their orders and making sure that there was still enough time to relax before Ken had to head to the departure gate, everyone exhaled.

Jasmine was the first to speak. "I am so sorry, Mom. I knew you had my best interest at heart, but I thought I had it all under control. I finally got the help that I needed when I almost lost Ethan to the system," Jasmine said in between sobs.

Mabel did not want to say the wrong thing. Her silence was confirmed when she caught Ken's eyes and he gently shook his head. So, Mabel just held Jasmine's hands and listened.

It was obvious that she was doing much better. Her sunken blue eyes now looked captivating. She also looked less gaunt and was not on edge like she constantly was before. There was a softer look to her, which made her seem relaxed. She had grown her hair out and she looked radiant.

Ken could not help but wonder how she got to this point, and he wanted to know. His thoughts drifted to how it all started and as if on cue, Jasmine started to tell her story.

She had become addicted to pain medication, after an unfortunate accident at work had resulted in surgery. She was functional for a while and able to hide it, until her mom noticed some changes in her. Her speech was always jumbled, she was becoming increasingly forgetful, and she was hopping from one doctor to the next.

As a result of her behaviour, she got suspended from work, which caused her to spiral even more out of control.

Their mom's constant interference and tough love did not help the matter much. Jasmine said she felt judged and suffocated, which was why she cut ties with their mom and Ken.

Of course, it was not long before Jasmine's husband also left. He gave up after she kept disappearing. He said he was tired of her mood swings and could not be sure that she would kick her addiction habit. He accepted a job offer in Australia and moved away without a word, not even for Ethan. Jasmine found out when she was on her way to drop Ethan off at school, one fateful morning. He left a letter on the kitchen counter.

"Remi's support was unwavering," Jasmine continued, speaking about her best friend from nursing school. Ken nodded gently in a bid to encourage her to continue.

Jasmine said she hit rock bottom and was at risk of being evicted and losing Ethan. It was then that she knew she needed to get help.

"What do you mean you were at risk of losing Ethan," Ken asked, "what happened?"

"I forgot to pick him up from school one day, I was just so tired and a little drugged that I passed out cold at home. Remi was the one who went and got him. I had already been issued three formal warnings for picking Ethan up late or, sometimes, not at all. The next event was going to lead to children's services becoming involved.

Opening the front door in a hazy fog, after hearing faint sounds of someone banging on my door, for several minutes, there stood Remi and Ethan soaking wet from the heavy rain......."

Jasmine choked back the tears. Her mother reached across the table and rubbed Jasmine's hand.

"I knew then that I needed to get help, and quickly. I could not lose Ethan."

Jasmine looked at her son who was sitting close to Ken. Ken was playing with him to distract him from hearing his mother's story, even though he was aware that Ethan had seen more than a child his age should ever see about his mother.

Even after she sought help, Jasmine still felt unclean compared to her parents and Ken. After all, they were Christians and she felt inadequate in comparison. She always felt like she never came close to her parents' and Ken's accomplishments. They were good people and had constantly sacrificed their time in volunteer and missionary work. Ken and her parents constantly told her how proud they were of her work as a chemotherapy nurse, but her insecurities kept eating away at her.

Her choice of husband didn't help either, as he constantly spoke down at her, especially when she put on weight after childbirth and after her back surgery. Max would compare her to his female colleagues at work. When she was off work and not in uniform, he constantly wanted her in dresses and skirts, and her hair a certain way. He would complain about how she ate and spoke at his work dinners. Honestly, it was exhausting.

It was probably a good thing that he left anyway as she had never felt strong enough to leave him and he didn't do much for her confidence, if anything, he chipped away gradually at it until she became a shadow of herself.

She always thought she struck luck when he asked her out and then asked her to marry him. Now, with counselling, she understood that he was a control freak, who never loved her.

"All he did was prey on my vulnerability to make himself feel better," Jasmine said, dabbing at her eyes with a napkin.

"Jasmine, honey, why didn't you tell me any of this? It would have helped me to understand what you were going through," Mabel said, breaking her silence. Seeing her daughter cry was more than she could handle.

"I was ashamed. You and dad and Ken were always so perfect," Jasmine explained.

"Oh, do not say that. I am not perfect, and neither was your father. And Ken is surely not perfect either. Where on earth did you get that from?"

"From seeing your life with dad. How much he loved you, how much you loved each other. I wanted that too and I thought I had found it in Max."

Ken sat quietly. In his mind, he was pondering his own failed relationship with Bibi. Was it impossible to have today, the kind of relationship his parents had shared? Did people not love like that anymore?

His mother reached across the table and touched Jasmine's hand. "I never expected you or any of my children to be perfect. To want that would mean that I am perfect, and God knows I have made some mistakes."

"Thanks, mom," Jasmine said, feeling her heart heal a little bit.

Mabel nodded. "So, is everything okay now? Are you and Ethan safe?"

Jasmine nodded. "Telling you both my story is part of my recovery process."

Ken got up and hugged his sister. He could not believe everything she had gone through, and without having her family's support.

After a second, Jasmine lovingly pulled away. "Ken, I am not going to break, I am glad to be doing this. My recovery journey started through an outpatient rehabilitation centre, the very next day after the last time I forgot to pick Ethan up from school. There were bad days and good days, and days when I almost gave up. Coming back home to Ethan always reminded me of why I had to persevere."

"On my bad days, Remi was round in a flash, sometimes even taking Ethan for the night. I am still working my way through the programme and proud of how far I have come."

Working things through with her mom, especially, was now an integral part of her recovery and she was glad that Ken had taken the bold step of contacting her. She would be forever grateful to him.

Ken had tried ringing her several times, but the phone number he had for Jasmine was disconnected. He did not give up on finding her. Instead, he took a leap of faith and decided to go to the hospital where she had worked as a chemotherapy nurse before her suspension. At the hospital, he ran into a mutual friend who told him that Jasmine's suspension had been conditional, and she had fulfilled all that was needed from her, so she now worked in a health centre nearer to her home.

At the health centre, Ken left a letter with his mom's details and his travel itinerary, hoping that she would make contact. And she had done more than make contact, here she was at the airport to see him off and share what had happened to her with her family.

Ken was glad.

* * *

Ken looked at his watch. He had just enough time to hug and kiss them all before sprinting through the security checkpoint to international departures.

"Thank you for initiating contact, Ken. I know you must go, or you'll miss your flight, but I just wanted you to know that I picked up the phone so many times to ring Mom, and you too, but I was so ashamed of my behaviour that I just couldn't."

Mabel took her daughter's hands in hers as she rose from her seat. Jasmine followed her mom's lead and stood up too.

"It is all water under the bridge, it was not you, it was the addiction. Let us start over please, I made my mistakes too. I could have managed things better."

"I would love that, Mom."

Ken reluctantly stood up. It was nice seeing this moment of reconciliation right before he was heading out on his mission, but if he did not leave now, he could miss his flight.

"I really have to go now," he said, looking from his mother to his sister. "Jasmine, we have a lot of catching up to do. I know mom will fill you in, but I have got to run now."

He reached over to Ethan and pulled his nephew to his side, ruffled his hair before kneeling to hug him. Then he hugged his mother and his sister, said goodbye, and headed off towards the security checkpoint. Bibi briefly crossed his mind as he made his way through the fast-moving line.

His steps felt heavy, although he was also exhilarated at what had just happened to his family. He wished he were not leaving, but it was too late to turn back.

After going through the security checkpoint, Ken retrieved his headphones from his neck and secured them firmly over his ears, then with a final backward glance, he waved at his family as he rounded the corner and headed towards his departure gate.

CHAPTER 12

The last several weeks had been torturous for Bibi. She could hardly think straight, and she craved his presence and voice daily. She had noticed his absence from church, the last three Sundays since the last time she was there. And as much as she did not want to admit it, his absence was affecting her singing.

She did not even feel like attending choir practice anymore and getting out of bed in the mornings had become a chore. It was almost as if she lived in her dressing gown now because she hardly bothered with her appearance at home any longer.

She had not realised how much Ken had meant to her until recently. He had been her everything. Hence, she could not understand why it was so easy for him to cut her off and stay away for this long.

Over the last few weeks, Bibi had gone through every range of emotion possible: from anger to heartbreak to anxiety to fear.

Her parents would be arriving for her graduation in a week; she was not looking forward to it. She just wanted her Ken.

As a distraction, she now volunteered at the Citizen Advice Bureau twice a week. She had been to his apartment and rang his phone repeatedly but to no avail. It was as if he had just vanished off the surface of the earth.

The only thing getting her through her days was Naomi's constant presence. Naomi had come around every single day since the day she found out. She cleaned, she cooked, she made jokes, she gossiped, all to cheer Bibi up. She was bringing food and groceries and exhibiting the patience of a saint. Although Bibi was grateful to have Naomi, and usually enjoyed her company, there were still days when she would rather not have her around. Today was one such day. Knowing Naomi so well though, Bibi knew that Naomi was not one to easily give up on her loved ones.

Bibi got off her sofa and was heading to the bathroom when she heard a knock at the door. She had been thinking of giving Naomi a key since she practically lived there now, but she kept forgetting to make a copy. She only went out on days when it was necessary now, and there were so many other worries on her mind, it was no wonder that she kept forgetting.

"Are you still in your dressing gown, Bibi?" Naomi asked scoldingly, as soon as Bibi let her in.

"I was on my way to freshen up when you knocked, Naomi," Bibi said, sounding a bit irritated. Naomi was slowly making her way from friend to mother and today was not the day for criticism. She had gotten out of bed that morning feeling worse for wear.

"It's okay, Bibi," Naomi said, her voice much softer than before. "Today, I brought lunch, you and I are going to talk it out, come up with a plan, a way forward - together."

Bibi looked at her with a blank stare.

"You go and freshen up. I'll get everything set so we can eat when you come back out."

Bibi did not want to argue, so she headed to the bathroom to freshen up. A fresh change of clothes and she felt a little better. When she came back out, Naomi had laid out a spread on the dining table and was scrolling through her phone. She quickly hid the phone when Bibi appeared.

"Was that him?" Bibi asked.

"Him who?" Naomi asked.

"Don't do that, Naomi. You know who I mean," Bibi said, her eyes glistening with tears.

"No, Bibi. No. That was not him. I already promised you, if or when I hear from him, you will be the first one to know."

"So, are you telling me the truth, that he has not reached out to you? That you do not know where he is?"

Naomi nodded sadly. "I'm telling you the truth, Bibi. I'm sure he's staying away from me because he's trying to keep me out of the middle. Does it hurt me? Yes. Do I understand why he's doing things this way? Absolutely. I'm mad though! And when he shows his face back here, you know I'm going to give him an earful".

Naomi got up and pulled out a chair for Bibi to sit down. Bibi smiled faintly.

"Look at us, we're like a married couple," Naomi joked.

Bibi chuckled.

Dishing out plates of food, Naomi continued. "I know the hurt you're going through, Bibi. Not that this compares, but when my father cut me off because I revealed my sexuality to him and my mom, I thought I was going to die. It was the hardest choice I have ever had to make in my life ... choosing between my dad and what I stood for. It cost me my relationship with my father, the man I was sure would be in my corner."

Bibi rubbed Naomi's arm. "Do you think about him?"

"Every day of my life. What I remember most are the summers I spent with him in Haiti. We used to have such fun times together. I guess that was because he saw me as his little girl then."

Naomi paused, took a sip of water while Bibi continued rubbing her shoulder, encouraging her to go on.

"One day, I was always welcome to visit him in Haiti, I was his little girl, his Mimi; the next day, I was all sorts of names I would not repeat. He said he needed time to wrap his head around things before I could visit again. That invitation is yet to come."

"Are you hopeful that things can change, that things will get better, that he'll come to see his mistake?"

"Sure. There is always hope. He is my father, and I did not do anything so terrible to him besides accept myself for who I am. We do talk from time to time, but I'm mostly the one doing the calling. Regardless, I'm happier and free now, no more secrets, it was eating me up inside."

They ate in silence for a minute, then Bibi broke the silence.

"He's most likely gone back into the missionary field," Bibi said, breaking the silence.

"Huh? What?"

"He mentioned briefly once that there was a missionary trip to Uganda coming up, but he was not sure if he was going to go. I think he decided to go after all."

"Oh. That is possible, yes."

They fell back into silence. Bibi moved the food around in her plate, staring at nothing in particular.

"I think it's time for me to move on."

Naomi dropped her fork and looked up from her plate.

"How do you mean?"

"I'm cutting my losses and moving back home. Over the last few weeks, I've been dreading the arrival of my parents at my graduation, but I've been thinking lately, that it's time to go back home with them. There's nothing left for me here."

Naomi winced.

"No, I don't mean it that way. You know what I mean."

Naomi nodded sadly, while Bibi looked out in the distance.

"I'll start life afresh, do what's expected of me. This is over. It's all over. Maybe I can be happy now."

CHAPTER 13

Bibi was all packed up and ready to go. The day was finally here, and she was moving to her parents' house in Kent. The plan was for her to live there until her parents arrive for her graduation, and then together, after her graduation, they would all leave and head to Nigeria. The thought of living in Kent filled Bibi with nostalgia. She had spent the better part of her summer holidays in England in this historic, south-eastern county.

She looked around her apartment and felt a tug at her heart. She had many memories here; she could not believe that she was leaving it all behind. Aside from her toiletries and necessities which she had left out, there was a picture frame of her and Ken sitting on her bedside table. Naomi had taken the picture without warning, the last time that she and Ken had gone to visit his mom on her birthday. In the picture, Ken was looking at her whilst she was looking away. She loved how it captured the longing and love in Ken's eyes.

Bibi remembered it as a beautiful day. Naomi's mom had also been there, and all together, the five of them had enjoyed an impromptu picnic in Ken's mother's garden. Later, Ken confessed to her that the day could have been better if his sister were there. He looked sad when he shared that with her. Bibi knew that he was estranged from his sister and that it had something to do with their mom, but he had not gone into details. Looking back now, she wondered if she should have asked more questions, been more interested, probed more? She couldn't even remember his sister's name; did she even ask for her name or anything about her? She had really been selfish! Shaking her head she smirked, as she relished in her thoughts.

The following week, on Bibi's birthday, Ken had given her a copy of that picture. It sat beautifully in a rustic, wooden, antique frame. She hadn't given the picture much thought in the months that followed, but looking at it now, it meant the world to her. It was exquisite! Ken's boyish grin revealed his dimple, making him look ravishing.

She planned to wrap it up as a parting gift to him. She would add a card and drop it off at his mother's house. She was sure he was not at his mom's house, but she could not leave the UK without seeing her. Moreover, she needed to feel close to Ken.

Ken always said the picture was his favourite of them together. He wanted to make a copy for himself but never got around to doing so. She didn't need any pictures to remember him, despite the numerous ones on her phone, she would always carry him in her heart.

* * *

Rather than taking the bus to the train station, Bibi decided to walk. She needed to clear her head. She was in no hurry as she strolled, cutting through the local park. She had sent her bags ahead of her to Kent, with a transportation service.

Bibi stopped briefly by the pond and watched the gentle ripple of waves created by a duck and her ducklings, as they waddled across. It was a beautiful sight to behold! Two joggers ran by and nodded at her. She smiled in response and kept walking at a steady pace. She loved the idea of exercising but lacked the willpower to get into it.

When she came to a row of shops, she stopped. Her local café was just a few doors down and the smell of fresh-brewed coffee had awakened something in her brain. Like a robot being controlled by an outside force, she went in and ordered. Then she went and stood to one side of the counter as she waited for her order. She was looking out the window, engaged in her favourite pastime, when Ken walked right past the café.

She ran to the door and looked around frantically, but he had disappeared. This had been happening a lot. Was it her mind playing tricks on her? Was it a mirage? Was she really going mad? Pining for Ken was all she had been doing the last couple of days.

Feeling defeated once again, she walked back to collect her drink as the barista called out her name. Bibi's eyes dropped to the array of pastries on display, and she just could not resist. But with a quick check of the time on her phone, she was disheartened to realise there was such a short window of time to catch her train. With an inward groan, she hurried to the train station. Thankfully, she just about made it, panting and all. Maybe, she really did need to exercise. Finally, she sat on the train sipping her cappuccino and looking out of the window, watching towns and landscapes scurrying by. She wondered if she had made the right decision to visit Ken's mom, but even if the answer was no, it was too late now.

Bibi adjusted herself in the seat to make herself comfortable, then she retrieved her phone from her handbag and plugged in her earphones. Then she let her mind drift to her most recent conversation with Maya.

"Abisola!"

Just the sheer fact that Maya had called her by her full name and not her pet name rattled her cage. She already had a feeling that this dialogue was not going to go her way.

"All I have heard is how you feel and what he has done to you, what of how Ken feels? Why does it have to be all about you and how you have been hurt?" Maya's words cut through her, and her blood ran cold. But she was not even done yet, just getting started as it would seem.

"When are you going to start making decisions for yourself? At least one that is this important? Marriage is a lifetime journey, and you are going to be the one living with whomever you settle down with. Ken has feelings too and he is human. Yes, he loves you and is willing to compromise, but what exactly do you want? Do you really love him?" A slight pause followed.

"Personally, I don't know many guys that would have hung around that long, at least he tried," Maya pointed out.

"Clearly, you don't know the right men then," Bibi muttered under her breath.

"I will pretend I didn't hear that sass," Maya said and continued. *"A man is professing love for you, and you continue to hide*

him like he is a leper or worse. Tell me, how exactly did you think this would play out?"

"But you know my parents, the thought of disobeying them scares me. It is just not worth the hassle," Bibi replied cautiously.

"Are you going to be tied to your parents' aprons forever because you are an only child?"

Bibi's thoughts were interrupted by the loud horns of the speeding train. She looked around the cabin and everyone's head was buried in some kind of device. Only a handful of them were reading newspapers and books. Bibi smiled at how much the world had not changed since her last train ride. Nobody noticed anybody anymore.

"I am thinking that perhaps it is the thought that they may cut you off like they have threatened to do, that scares you. You know that they will do it, should you go against their wishes. On the other hand, could it be the fact that you will miss them or the luxurious lifestyle to which you are accustomed?" Maya asked.

Bibi winced on the phone but did not respond. A part of her knew that Maya was right.

"We grew up together and you have done everything their way, from your career to your choice of clothes, to your vocations. They have lived their dreams through you, where do you draw the line?"

"Why are you exaggerating, what vocations?" Bibi snapped back.

"For starters, you wanted to take singing lessons, but your mom insisted that you took tennis lessons instead. Again, you wanted to take piano lessons, your mom was adamant that you would benefit from ballet lessons which you hated with a passion. You only took

piano lessons when you attended law school and even then, you hid it from them."

Ouch, that hurt. Bibi was getting angry and defensive.

"At least, I didn't settle," she shot back, instantly regretting her outburst. Even before the words came out, she wanted to stop but could not. She was blinded by so much rage.

"Settle? That is what you think I did? Well, at least I settled for someone I chose. And yes, he is by no means perfect, but I am happy," Maya hurled back.

Conceding, Maya closed her eyes, counted to ten, and continued.

"Bibi, there is no need for us to get spiteful. I have nothing but love for you. I genuinely want you to be happy, however, if you rang me just so I can tell you that you have done everything right, I am sorry that I have disappointed you. Also, that will be untrue to you and what our relationship stands for. No matter what decision you make, I will always be here for you. I am not saying disobey your parents but let them know you have a voice too."

She paused, then in almost a whisper, said, *"I can hear Bobo waking up from his nap, catch up soon."*

* * *

As her train started to pull into Southend-on-Sea train station, Bibi realised she had been sobbing quietly. She pulled out her compact mirror and touched up lightly, trying to cover up the blotches all over her face.

"Can I get you anything?" the train attendant asked her.

"No thanks, I will be fine. I just need a few minutes," Bibi answered. She was a hot mess, and she knew it.

Pulling herself together, she disposed of her coffee cup and alighted the train.

✳ ✳ ✳

The sky was overcast with grey clouds by the time Bibi disembarked from the taxi. She removed a cash note from her back pocket and paid her fare, mumbling her thanks as she did so. When he tried to give her change, she asked him to keep it. Maybe it was guilt!

The taxi driver had tried to engage her in conversation, which was nice of him, but she just was not in the mood for small talk. She even put in her earphones at one point, but that did not stop him from talking. However, when he noticed that all he was getting were monosyllabic responses, he stopped. Normally, she would feel bad, but not today. All she wanted was quiet, was that too much to ask for?

Bibi walked up to the front door trying her best not to look despondent. She pressed the doorbell and waited. Inside, her heart was pumping rapidly. She rang the bell again. This time, she heard a shrill on the other side, and almost immediately the door swung open.

"You weren't supposed to meet me here! My car gave me away again, right?" the voice said, as soon as the door flung open. Bibi stood a few inches shorter than the gorgeous, blue-eyed, blond-haired woman who had just opened the door. Bibi was taken aback, as they both sized each other up.

It was now apparent why she had not been able to reach Ken. With her mind in overdrive, she suddenly felt on edge and could barely think straight. Clearly, Ken had moved on.

Why had she decided to wear this pair of jeans today? It was her favourite pair, but she was suddenly aware that they were faded, and her linen top was all creased up. Not a good representation of an ex-fiancé at all. Meanwhile, this beautiful lady standing before her looked put together in a burgundy top with balloon sleeves, a pair of ripped jeans, and stiletto shoes.

Tilting her head to one side as she felt the sudden onset of a headache, all those voices came flooding back into her head. They were the same voices that had clearly warned her over and over that she and Ken would not last.

Closing her eyes tightly, she hoped those voices would be silenced.

"Hello, how can I help you?"

Her voice brought Bibi back to the present. Bibi could barely speak, she stumbled on her words and all she could get out was, "I got the wrong house, I am so sorry to have disturbed you."

Not waiting for a response, Bibi hurriedly walked away, but not without apologising profusely again. Who was this woman? Not only was she gorgeous, but her voice was sultry too.

As Bibi walked away dabbing her tears, she noticed a car pull into the driveway next door and two ladies alighted from the car, the younger lady waved at the mysterious lady she had just met at Mabel's house.

"Nettie, how are you doing?"

"Oh, that is her name! Unique name too." Bibi thought

As Nettie went back to arranging the flowers that she had gotten for Mabel, she thought to herself "*Why would such a beautiful lady look so downcast and sad? She seemed to have been crying too.*"

Mabel had travelled into London for further medical tests and assessments, she had been referred by the local hospital.

CHAPTER 14

Ken stepped off the plane and made his way onto the jetway. He nodded his gratitude and smiled at the cabin crew by the door. Still thinking about Naomi's missed phone call right before take-off, he plodded on until he came to the travelator. There was a mom with about three bags, a baby strapped onto her back, and a toddler by her side. She seemed so unfazed by it all and he marvelled at her strength, and how she made it look so easy to manage.

Coming down the escalator into the immigration hall, the wave of heat that hit him was like none he had encountered before. From his travels, he had experienced extreme weather conditions, however, this time was different as he was mentally and physically drained. Instead of elation, he felt trepidation, he had been restless throughout the plane ride and had been unable to eat or sleep despite the weariness he felt. As he joined the queue for immigration, he could not help mulling over his decision and whether it was the right choice to make.

Maybe he should have answered Naomi's call, she would have been able to help him decide. He had been avoiding her just to avoid Bibi, but he was beginning to wonder if that had been the best approach. He hoped by ignoring Naomi, he was not at risk of losing her friendship. That would hurt him more than anything; it was not his intention.

"Next!"

Ken stood by impatiently as the immigration officer looked through his passport several times. *"Oga, how now? Wetin happen, any problem?"* Ken asked the officer in pidgin English.

The officer looked at him curiously and smiled before waving him on after stamping his passport. *"All this oyinbo people wey think say them sef don become one of us."* Shaking his head, he signalled to the next person to step forward.

Ken got through the rest of the airport quickly with nothing to declare nor any luggage to claim, he was on his way out of the main doors in no time.

Approaching the main door and just before he stepped out, he scanned the crowd for his friend. There were several placards with passengers' names on them. A young lady with a lanyard around her neck approached him and asked if he needed to purchase a SIM card. He declined the offer and she smiled and walked on. He took a few steps forward and was approached by another young lad who asked if he needed a taxi or needed to purchase the local currency. Again, with a polite smile, he shook his head.

Ladi was waiting for him right outside the exit. The two of them met on a missionary trip many years ago and had remained friends ever since. Ken knew if he had to be in Nigeria to see Bibi's father, then he would need Ladi's support. So, he called the week before, to tell Ladi of his plans. Ladi had been supportive and even offered to go with Ken to see Bibi's parents.

Ladi welcomed Ken with a hug. "Welcome to Nigeria, my friend! Let's go, lots to plan. This step is quite an audacious one," Ladi said in his jovial voice.

Ladi led the way across the busy street. Trying to converse as they walked was almost impossible because they were interrupted by taxi drivers trying to get them into their cabs, hawkers trying to sell them cold drinks and snacks, and money dealers trying to sell local currency. After what seemed like an eternity, they finally made it to the car park.

Ken had wanted Ladi to take him straight to Bibi's house, but Ladi had talked him down and insisted on another approach. It had not been an easy feat. Ken reluctantly took Ladi's advice to go home with him, so he could rest and feel refreshed the next day for the big event. But before then, they headed to the market to buy some items as gifts for Bibi's parents.

Ken was unable to sleep that night. He was up at the crack of dawn, ready to go, before Ladi woke up.

A few hours later, Ken and Ladi were dressed up in matching navy blue *Atiku* native attires, looking dashing and ready to work their charm. The short-sleeved tunics with matching trousers and light embroidery exuded simple elegance. Ken looked in the mirror and liked what he saw.

"Thank you for doing this," he said, smiling widely at Ladi. "These outfits look great."

Ladi responded with a chuckle. "Anytime my man, anytime."

"You are a man of great wisdom, Ladi. Thank you for walking me through how to properly go through this process."

"Well, I cannot take all the credit, man. It was my dad. I mentioned that you were coming, and why, and he schooled me on what was culturally right and wrong. Luckily though, mom had purchased this fabric last year for my brother and I, but we never got round to wearing them. It also helps that the three of us are of similar builds and close in body sizes."

Ken smiled and thanked Ladi again, for being so prepared.

"Let's get going," Ladi simply replied, "the earlier the better, so that we can beat the traffic."

The drive to Bibi's house was uneventful. The gifts, which one of the shop owners had neatly wrapped, were sitting in the back seat of Ladi's Audi A3.

Ken remembered the way the market women had fawned over him, and it brought back feelings of nostalgia from back when he had first visited Bibi's church before he became a regular worshipper there.

Ken settled back into the passenger's seat as Ladi manoeuvred his way to Bibi's childhood home. The place he had heard so much about. Ken was pensive but was enjoying the hustle and bustle, the loud and endless hooting of impatient drivers, and the calls of hawkers when traffic slowed or came to a standstill. The chaos dissipated as they drew closer to their intended destination. It felt like they had been catapulted into a different world. Less chaos on this side of town. It was quieter and slower paced. People were jogging and strolling on the sidewalks. A young couple held hands as they talked and giggled. It caused his heart to skip a beat, he missed this.

At the main gate to Bibi's parents' house, they were politely greeted and interrogated by a pair of uniformed men. Then they were kept waiting briefly while one of them communicated animatedly on the phone. Finally, they were let in. The never-ending driveway wound through a very scenic landscape with tasteful ornaments. Ken and Ladi looked around them quietly as Ladi drove on. After what seemed like an eternity, the driveway opened and there it was, the grandeur of it all. Mr and Mrs Ajayi's mansion. Ken's childhood home was modest in comparison to this.

Ken was in awe of the mansion before him.

Just before the car stopped, two uniformed ladies and a young lad, also in uniform, seemed to have been expecting them. The ladies curtsied and the lad bowed as they came out of the car. The lad took the car keys and the ladies brought out the gifts which had been beautifully packaged in three baskets and two boxes with matching ribbons. They were ushered into the lounge; the décor was well crafted and luxurious. Ken looked around nervously while they waited.

This property was certain to be worth millions, how could he possibly compete. He was clearly out of his league here. He felt himself begin to fidget, and he stuttered when one of the ladies came back to offer them refreshments. Ladi politely declined on their behalf. Despite the coolness in the room, Ken began to sweat. Then he remembered his uncle's prayers for him just as he and Ladi had set off to Bibi's house. They had spoken briefly over the phone. It calmed him and he began to relax again.

Just then, he felt a tap on his shoulder. He looked at Ladi as if just coming out of a trance. Ladi was motioning to Ken to follow him and the young lady who was now standing before them. Ken nodded and followed Ladi and the lady to the living room which was also exquisite in its design and décor.

As soon as they were seated, they heard footsteps approaching. Ladi gestured for Ken to stand with him. Bibi's mom closely followed Mr Ajayi as they came into the living room. As soon as they came into sight Ladi and Ken prostrated fully on the floor in reverence, both facing downwards.

"You are both welcome, please, stand up and sit." They both stood and Mr Ajayi shook their hands firmly before they took their seats. For a tall, imposing man, his voice did not seem to match him; silvery and soft-spoken. Bibi's dad proceeded to ask them about refreshments. Ladi again declined the offer. Ken looked at Bibi's mom out of the corner of his eyes. She was strikingly beautiful, just like her daughter, though she did not look pleased. Her body language was not encouraging nor welcoming at all. Her arms crossed defensively over her chest, she kept shaking her legs and she kept sighing. Even when he and Ladi greeted her directly, she answered them in undertones. This is crunch time, he had better get his A-game on, it was now or never.

"Eh, welcome," Bibi's father said once they were all comfortably seated, and he had asked them one last time about refreshments and Ladi had once again declined.

"So, I hear you wanted to talk to Bisola's mom and I."

"Yes sir," Ladi replied on their behalf. "Thank you for having us in your beautiful home."

Ken nodded in agreement.

"Please accept this token we have brought on behalf of my friend, Ken," Ladi continued as he pointed to the gifts, also bowing his head as a sign of respect. "He has something he would like to say to you. Over to you, Ken."

Ken edged forward in his seat and bowed his head slightly before speaking. "I have come to formally ask you for Bisola's hand in marriage sir."

Mr Ajayi didn't respond but acknowledged and encouraged him to speak further with a nod. Ken felt his shoulders relax and he exhaled internally, the vibe was good. But before he could continue, Mrs Ajayi's voice interrupted the vibe.

"Hand in marriage? Did you say her hand in marriage? Ah, ah, but she never mentioned you at all, this is like going from zero to hundred. *Abi ke!*"

Ken's back was up again. Just when he thought he was getting somewhere... His insides groaned, Ladi looked at him encouragingly.

Mr Ajayi placed his hand on his wife's arm as if to reassure her. "Dorcas, my wife......let's hear these young men out."

Then, it all happened so fast that Ken could hardly recollect the order of events.

"Hear them out! Are you saying I do not know my daughter at all?" She turned her attention to Ken, then almost immediately back to her husband.

Now standing, arms akimbo and a deep frown, "Did you even date her at all? What have you done to my daughter?" Bibi's mom was hysterical, even her husband looked stunned. Mrs Ajayi would not stop, at this point, she was almost incoherent.

Mr Ajayi looked defeated. "We will have to do this another time," he said, as he ushered his wife away.

Ken sank to the floor holding his head in his hands. Bibi was now out of his grip. Ladi tried to reassure him that all was not lost, but Ken could not see how this was not the end of the road.

"My guy," Ladi said to him, "you still have five more days in Nigeria. We will come back every day if we must."

Ken shook his head sadly. "It's not meant to be."

EPILOGUE

"Abisola, your dad and I thought it would be nice to have a lovely, intimate, family dinner tonight to celebrate your graduation before the actual ceremony."

Bibi looked at her mom, confused. She had just come downstairs for breakfast. Her parents had arrived days earlier than planned, and they were all staying at the family's holiday home in Kent.

"Mom, but why now? There is a big party planned to happen in Nigeria when we get back home, there is no need for all this fuss."

"Fuss, which one is fuss? Do you think you are in the court of law? Just because you are a law graduate does not mean you can start to question your parents! There will be one or two people around too, so look your best," her mom said, almost shouting at this point.

"Who are these people, Mom?" Bibi asked with so much dejection. Celebrating was the last thing on her mind.

"My dear daughter, just be ready. There will be a car here in an hour for you too." Bibi looked up, puzzled. Before Bibi could think of a comeback, her mom was walking out of the kitchen. She loved her mom, but she could be overbearing at times. It was always her way or the highway.

But she knew not to disobey her parents. So half-heartedly, Bibi sat down to eat breakfast after which she went up to her room to get ready while trying to think of an outfit for the dinner. She lacked enthusiasm, she just wanted to sleep but she dared not defy her mom.

Later that evening, after spending her day shopping and getting pampered at the spa, courtesy of her mother, Bibi started to get ready for the dinner ahead of her. She tried to think of who her mother had invited to the house but kept coming up empty. Most of the people her parents knew in UK were their own friends, people they met up with regularly, and no one Bibi's age, so she was wondering why her mother would invite her own friends to celebrate. They had cousins and relatives around, but she and her parents rarely saw them. Then jolting up, a thought crossed her mind, but she dismissed it quickly. Was this a setup, some sort of match-making scenario? Deep down she knew there was a strong possibility of this happening, and her heart sank.

Bibi sighed heavily as she slipped into her elegant black Louboutin slingbacks. Then she stood and ran her hand down her long red Balmain dress to smoothen out a few creases. If this was a setup, she'd better look good, she thought resignedly.

She thought back to when her mom asked her to meet her friend's son at Paddington train station, to pick up some necessities she had sent Bibi. Bibi was mystified, as she had not requested for anything to be sent. She went, all the same.

Tobi had a lovely manner about him, he was polite and well put together, even invited her to a nearby bistro for breakfast. At the end of that meeting, they parted amicably without exchanging numbers.

She had later checked the contents of the bag when she got home to find groceries she enjoyed from Nigeria, but she had been able to buy right there in London. Maybe her mom was just being thoughtful, missing her, or had merely just seized an opportunity.

It was when her mom rang her later that evening with so much excitement that she realised there had indeed been an agenda.

"Isn't Tobi a nice young man, when are you meeting again?"

"Meeting...for what now? He already gave me the things you sent," Bibi uttered, confused though.

"My daughter, did he not ask for your number or better still, did you not ask for his? He is an investment banker you know; he recently completed his master's in business administration about six months ago." It was then that it dawned on Bibi what had happened. She gave her excuses and hung up.

* * *

Bibi was greeted downstairs by Amah, her parents' housekeeper, who informed her that the guests had arrived and were gathered in the family room.

Deciding to bide her time before making her way to the family room on the second floor, where she knew her parents and their guests would be having drinks and making small talk before dinner, Bibi sat on the edge of the black leather sofa to collect her thoughts. She could hear afrobeat music playing softly in the background. She smiled; her parents sure knew how to live life to the fullest.

* * *

Bibi stood up and walked to the other end of the sitting room. In front of the heavy antique mirror hanging on the wall, she re-applied her Mac lip gloss before taking off her necklace, deciding it was a little too much. Her earrings and bracelet were just enough jewellery. She did not want her dress overshadowed; it made a statement of its own with the delicate sequined and pearl neckline.

Bibi felt her phone vibrate through her Valentino Garavani leather clutch and retrieved it. It was Naomi. She read Naomi's message with a grin and decided to respond before joining the shindig.

As she was putting her phone away, her mother's signature perfume floated through the air even before she heard her heels clicking noisily. Bibi braced herself as she turned around. She stepped back to admire her mom who swooped her into a tight embrace.

"Bisola, you look beautiful," her mom said as she held her at arm's length.

"Mom, you look gorgeous too," Bibi responded as she stood back to admire her exquisite peach lace boubou. The embroidery work around the neckline was simply to die for.

"You like?" her mom asked, smiling widely as she twirled around.

"Mom, I love!"

Truly, her mom looked graceful in her ensemble. There was no doubt that her makeup had been professionally done.

Probably by Ada, her mother's professional beautician, who lived not too far from their home in Kent.

"Was it Ada who tied your *gele*?" Bibi asked, admiring her mother's head-tie.

"Yes o, and I asked her to touch up my face lightly. After all, it is your night, and I do not want to upstage you."

Bibi laughed heartily. Trust her mom to downplay every-thing, even the obvious.

"Let's join the others in the family room, everyone has been waiting for you. You will not believe who we have here waiting to see you."

Bibi knew it would be fruitless to ask her mother who, so she simply followed her; she would just have to wait to see for herself.

Bibi walked behind her mother and past numerous chaffing dishes, lined up for the buffet that was to follow. Adjacent to the spread was the formal dining room. The transformation was styl-ish. There with a long table with chairs on both sides, and a black runner on the table. Placed on the runner were high vases with large lit white candles. Right in the middle of the table was a lily flowerpot. Each setting had silverware placed on white napkins, with white dining plates and crystal drinking glasses. The room was tastefully decorated in black and gold, and a banner hung up high on the wall, with her picture and inscription which simply read, *Congratulations Bibi.*

She could tell her mother was set on playing this game till the very end. Her mom turned to the left and she followed. They ascended the stairs to an oak door and came to a stop. Bibi could hear people chatting from behind the closed door.

As she stood to her mom's side, she became nervous. What kind of party had her mother planned? She looked at her mom who encouraged her to go in.

Bibi hesitated and then pushed the door open. She slowly made her way in.

She immediately recognized a few faces. There were friends of her parents, cousins and, from the corner of her eyes she saw him. Bibi froze. She had to steady herself by leaning on her mom.

Their eyes locked from across the room, just as they had, that first day that they met at Naomi's house party. He smiled and Bibi wanted to run across the room to embrace him and never let him go. Then the questions began to flood her mind. Ken was here... in the same room as her parents... in their home. How did this happen? She needed a pinch, this was not a dream, right? Ken walked towards her. She spotted his mom and Naomi on either side of him. They were all smiling. She still was not sure what to do with her face, she was happy yet confused.

Then she saw her! But what was she doing here with Ken?

The look on her face must have given away her jumbled thoughts because Ken was now standing in front of her, introducing the strange woman. The gorgeous blond woman!

"Bibi, meet my sister, Jasmine."

"Your sister? Your sister!" Bibi exclaimed, looking at Jasmine and shaking her hand. She heaved a sigh of genuine relief. It was a nostalgic moment as Bibi collapsed into his arms weeping.

"But you were called Nettie the day I came to the house" Bibi commented, her voice barely audible.

"That was my nickname in school. I played netball and apparently could net a ball from a respectable distance. I was in the same class as Mrs Heyward's niece, mom's neighbour" Jasmine replied humbly.

When she was finally able to, Bibi smiled again at Jasmine and embraced her. After speaking to Ken's mom, saying hello to Naomi, and giving her a tough time for not warning her about this surprise, Ken took Bibi to a corner of the room and fetched her a drink. Bibi needed to sit; it was all too much.

"I am sure you have so many questions, you clearly look over-whelmed. Let me just start by saying this: You were not joking when you mentioned how dramatic your mom can be. Phew, I experienced it first-hand! But it was all worth it. I will answer all your questions later, but right now, can we enjoy this moment with our families. As it turns out, this is not only your graduation dinner but our engagement dinner if you will still have me."

Bibi's heart and head were still unable to connect with what was happening around her. She was trying to make sense of every-thing that was happening. This could only be good, right!

Realisation suddenly set in. Their families were all together in one room. It was time to relax and ask questions later. Bibi smiled as she looked at Ken, their eyes held as he leaned forward to kiss her. Bibi closed her eyes; she had missed his soft lips and glorious smell. It was like time stood still for a moment, their lips locked in a slow rhythm and their arms entwined in a sweet magical embrace. Reluctantly, Ken pulled away from her gently. Standing up, he reached for Bibi's hand, and she took it with pride. With a twinkle in her eyes and a renewed spring in her step, she walked alongside him to re-join their families and friends to celebrate.

* * *

Putting the last two boxes in the truck, Ken spoke briefly to the young estate agent, Tom, who had arrived to put up the for-sale sign in front of his mother's house. Then, he went back inside where he found Jasmine and Bibi in the kitchen.

Jasmine was sitting on a low stool, heavily pregnant. He and Jasmine looked sadly at one another. Ken sighed heavily. This was his home, his place of affirmation and comfort. He could not believe they were selling it.

Jasmine was trying to hold it all together. Pushing herself off the stool, she waddled through the kitchen to the hallway and looked around for a few minutes before going off to the restroom.

After Jasmine left, Bibi hugged Ken and laid her head on his chest. Even after all this time, it felt so good to hold him close. She could feel his heart beating out of sync. It sounded broken and sad.

Ken had been trying all morning to stay upbeat, but she knew better. Packing up his mom's house, the place where he had grown up and spent most of his life, had to be emotionally draining for him and Jasmine.

Mabel's diagnosis had finally come back almost a year ago, and she was right, she had dementia. Of course, the diagnosis was sad, but it was such a relief to finally know what they were dealing with. They had decided that it was best if they lived close to Ken's mom to support her as she continued to live as independently as possible. It also meant they would be close to Jasmine, her partner, Alex, and her son, Ethan, who had recently decided to move as a family. They would be closer to the retirement village they had found for Mabel in their area. They could all visit her at a moment's notice and visit each other too. Ken was especially thrilled to be spending a lot more time with Ethan, and Bibi adored watching the two of them together.

Bibi took Ken's hand in hers and intertwined their fingers so she could see their matching wedding bands. The wedding had been small and intimate, held at the church they both attended in London, against her mother's wishes and just the way she wanted it. She had meant it when she pledged to be by his side forever, through the ups and the downs. This was their first down as husband and wife, and she was going to make sure that she made this as easy on him as possible.

Dementia was a new world to Bibi but learning about the disease itself helped her to understand the condition better. Initially, Mabel managed quite well, but when her short-term memory got worse, she needed more support. Bibi was also learning about patience, especially when it came to communicating with Mabel.

Having support through countless healthcare professionals and local support groups, made it all manageable though.

Seeing Mabel and the progression of her dementia made her often think back to Maya's father, her uncle Joe. He had died a while back, but Bibi just could not shake off how uncanny it was that he and Mabel, sometimes shared the same symptoms. It was beginning to dawn on her that Uncle Joe may have had dementia, although he was never formally diagnosed. It may have not been dementia after all, but now they would never know.

Ken and Jasmine had initially resisted the idea of moving their mother to a retirement village, but safety was becoming an issue. Mabel had once left an empty pot on the gas cooker; she had wanted to cook breakfast but completely forgot about it. The fire alarm was set off but luckily, there was no harm done.

Then just last week, she was found wandering the main street barefooted, with her bag hanging over her shoulder, a shopping list, and clothing unsuitable for the cold frosty weather.

Ken and Bibi had contemplated moving in with her, but she had been adamant and even had it in writing that she did not want to live with any of her children or vice versa, in the event of her deterioration. They had their own lives ahead of them. Mabel had even planned and paid for her own funeral. She made all her wishes clear, shortly after her diagnosis. So, they had no choice but to let her continue to live by herself in a retirement village, where she would have support from onsite staff.

When the last of the boxes had been loaded, Ken walked outside with Bibi by his side, followed closely by Jasmine and Ethan. Ken locked the front door and handed the key to Tom. He looked over at Jasmine who had tears in her eyes, and nodded reassuringly, letting her know that everything was going to be okay. Then, looking down at Bibi, whom he was now holding close, he smiled at her and said, "to new beginnings."

"To new beginnings," Bibi replied. She did not know what the future held for them, but she knew she was going to live every moment to the fullest because she had Ken by her side.

ABOUT THE AUTHOR

Ola grew up loving books. Some of her favourite series as a child included The Buttercup Series, The Famous Five, Secret Seven, Pacesetters, and The Babysitter's Club. She was nicknamed 'book worm' by one of her cousins and remembers getting mostly books for her 10th birthday. Not that it was a problem, she loved reading the books.

Ola had always hoped to write a book one day but never got round to it, until now of course.

She is a trained healthcare professional and has been fortunate to live on four continents. Her guilty pleasures include listening to inspirational podcasts and watching crime/law-based television programs. When she is not conversing with God, reading, or cooking, she loves nothing more than to hang out with the loves of her life; her husband and their three children.

This is her first novella; she enjoyed the gruelling process so much that she is already working on a sequel.

A Note from the Publisher

Thank you for buying this book. If you enjoyed reading it, you can help spread the word and support independent publishing by doing the following:

Recommend it. Suggest this book to your friends, pass it on, or buy it as a gift for someone. You can also suggest it to your book club or reader groups.

Talk about it. Mention it on Facebook, Instagram, Twitter or TikTok. Create a conversation about it. You can talk about it or review it on your blog. You may also use the cover image as your profile picture on social networking sites.

Review it. Leave a review online. It's easy to rate and leave reviews on retailers and other book websites.

Thank you for helping us to spread the word.

Accomplish Press
www.accomplishpress.com